C000178949

About the Author

I married young and travelled the world for over twenty years with my soldier husband. The jobs I did over that time were varied. When most people are looking to work towards their pension, I took four years out to achieve a BSc Hons (2:1) in Information and Communication Technology and Maths and a Post Graduate Course in Education (Primary). My new career in teaching culminated in headship.

In retirement, although writing has been my main focus, I do work for my church, I walk, swim, do tai chi and attend groups with the University of the Third Age (U3A).

The Secret Spy Struggles On

Lynne Pearson

The Secret Spy Struggles On

Olympia Publishers
London

www.olympiapublishers.com
OLYMPIA PAPERBACK EDITION

A CIP catalogue record for this title is
available from the British Library.

ISBN: 978-1-78830-562-4

This is a work of fiction.
Names, characters, places and incidents originate from the writer's
imagination. Any resemblance to actual persons, living or dead, is
purely coincidental.

First Published in 2020

Olympia Publishers
Tallis House
2 Tallis Street
London
EC4Y 0AB

Printed in Great Britain

Dedication

To G, my rock.

Acknowledgements

Jane's Defence Weekly for their informative articles on chemical agents.

Chapter One

Mustafa Younan was sitting in his cellar; so still, you would have thought him a statue. He was deep in thought, considering his next action. Less than a week ago, in this very same cellar, he had finished the construction of two ricin bombs. Using a sealed cabinet stolen from a science lab and wearing a new Nuclear Biological and Chemical (NBC) suit, and a high-quality respirator, he had inserted ricin into the shell of the bombs: in this case, two Nalgene bottles, egg timers, plywood, nails, wires, batteries and quick matches were all utilised to make the two bombs. The risky part had been putting the ricin into the bottles. Mustafa had taken no chances; after all, it was his own health and safety that he was worried about. The bombs had been handed over to Abdul-Azeem Tawfeek at the Zakaria Masjd Mosque. Mustafa didn't know where the bombs were to be planted, neither did he care. He had been doing that important job for the Prophet and he was very proud that he had done what he'd been asked.

Why was he so pensive then? Mustafa hadn't heard from Tawfeek since the meeting at the mosque. He hadn't heard anything on the news about bombs exploding, so what had Tawfeek done with them? These questions kept rolling around in Mustafa's brain and he thought he might be driven mad by them. His dilemma was that he'd been given a timetable. From the huge amount of castor beans that had been bought, a substantial amount of ricin had already been processed using everyday solvents and tools, such as mason jars and coffee filters. Mustafa had found it relatively easy to make ricin, his pleasure increasing with the knowledge that the tiniest amount could be fatal. Nausea, vomiting and then kidney and liver failure were all part of its charm for him. Particularly when it was killing unbelievers! The timetable given to him verbally by Tawfeek outlined the schedule for future bomb production. Accordingly, the date Mustafa had been instructed to start making three more bombs was today. Should he begin the process, or should he wait for Tawfeek to contact him first? The image of Tawfeek's face flashed into Mustafa's mind, an image so clear he could again feel the palpitations of his heart. The red, angry eyes and the edge to Tawfeek's voice when instructing Mustafa not to tell anyone about his bomb making skills, made him go cold with fear. His decision now made, construction of the two new bombs would begin without further deliberation. Mustafa realised he'd be able to make these bombs more quickly because he was now confident with the process. Abdul-Azeem Tawfeek would be happy about that, he thought.

***

Adrian Smythe was sitting in his office at Specialised Security Systems in London. His company legitimately provided security systems for anyone who cared to buy them. The company was, however, a good cover for the work Adrian did to keep the country safe. Questions were rolling around in his head too. Was the radicalisation of young men in the Zakaria Masjd Mosque still continuing? Who'd made the ricin bombs?

Were there any more planted in Sweden or in any other countries? Where were the castor beans being stored and processed? They'd had some good fortune identifying the Fighters for Freedom (FfF) website through which coded messages were being sent about the prospective bombing, but they may not have the same luck in the future. It had been a couple of days since they'd found the bombs and Adrian knew the war against terrorism was far from over. Sporting a lovely black eye, or should I say blue, purple and green eye from where he'd fallen a few days before and still with a dull ache in his head, Adrian was trying to ignore his symptoms. A plan was needed and he knew he would have to have the outline for that plan before the end of the day when he was to facetime with the PM. With a sigh, Adrian settled down to work.

***

Alison Andrews, Ali to everyone but her parents, had slept for twelve hours yet she felt drained. She had been through a plethora of emotions over the past few days and was now feeling the effects. Ali had been recruited to help her country because of her excellent skills with computers and technology. Sounds a bit 007? Ali would not have been your idea of a spy. A retiree who kept herself fit with various activities including tai chi, swimming, walking and much more, as well as having an active presence as Ninja Nanny on gaming sites such as Minecraft (Survival Mode) and Clash of Clans, Ali had an innate curiosity so was an ideal candidate for intrigue. Her perusal of the Dark Web and its many forks and joins was purely to satisfy this curiosity; she had no intention of using any of the services she found there. However, she was very careful to activate software she'd written before she went onto the Dark Web and different software after she came off the site so her IP address couldn't be traced back to her. She also had a different name for that — pi235711. Anonymity was key she believed. It was, however, her presence online that had been a contributory factor in stopping the planting and detonation of the ricin bombs in Sweden. Now, Ali wandered listlessly around her house, without a sense of purpose. She was feeling lost and unsure how to get back on an even keel, if she ever could get back to how she'd been before.

Her husband, Dan, had been unforthcoming about his relationship with Adrian Smythe when she'd challenged him. Adrian was someone they'd come across in 1978 when they were visiting Supreme Headquarters Allied Forces Europe and with whom they hadn't had any contact since, as far as she knew! However, when Ali had been working with Adrian, he had inadvertently mentioned Dan being away, on more than one occasion and Ali couldn't work out how he'd known; unless Dan was working for him, or unless the comments weren't inadvertent? Frustrating!

"Need to know," was Dan's answer to Ali when she questioned him.

They'd always had an agreement about what need to know meant, especially when Dan was a serving soldier, often undercover, but Ali still felt cross that she couldn't get an answer to her question this time. She wasn't one to give up so she would just have to find a different way to get the information she needed. At the moment, Ali wasn't exactly sulking, but she was making it plain that she wasn't happy. Dan seemed oblivious to the coolness and just carried on as normal, which Ali found even more annoying. Such is life, she thought to herself. Ali loved Dan and she knew she shouldn't be annoyed, but she was. Nobody said you had to be reasonable all the time, did they?

"I'm going for a ride, Ali. You interested?" Dan's voice broke through her reverie.

It only took a few seconds for Ali to answer.

"Sounds like a good idea. I'll be ready in five."

"Five would be a miracle," Dan chuckled to himself as he strolled into the garage where he would begin his routine check on his bike. He was well into his check when Ali appeared, dressed in her Lycra shorts and top.

"I will just give mine a quick check this time as I've been using it a fair bit while you've been away. Yours obviously needed a fuller check as you've not used it in a while."

Dan nodded in agreement, head bent over his back tire that had needed some air.

"Done!" Dan stated after a couple of minutes, as he stood up and stretched.

Ali handed Dan a hat, which he surveyed with some disdain.

"You know I don't wear those hats. They make me look like a peanut!"

"Safer though," Ali replied.

"I'll take my chances."

Ali let out a sigh, but she knew there was no point making an issue of it. Dan wouldn't wear a hat and that was that. He'd said before that we all make choices and not wearing a hat was his. He knew he'd said that he was responsible for any repercussions because of those choices. No answer to that really.

Ali took the lead initially, but Dan soon overtook her. He

liked to push the bike more than she did and she was happy to ride in his slipstream — a bit easier on the legs. Within minutes, Ali was feeling energised. Cycling always did this to her. She'd started cycling later in life and found it very hard at first but, now, she could get a good workout and feel the benefits for hours. Of course, she could also feel a few more twinges too, but she felt they were worth the effort. Head down, legs pumping and the breeze caressing her face gave Ali that feeling of peace and calmness that could be so difficult to find in the busy world in which she lived. Focussed on what she was doing, Ali didn't realise that Dan was slowing down so she almost ran into the back of his bike. Just in time she stopped.

"Get you next time!" she squealed as she stood on her brakes.

"Sorry, Ali, I forgot you were behind me. I should have been paying more attention," Dan replied.

"No harm done."

Both Dan and Ali got off their bikes and sat at the side of the road on the grassy bank enjoying a drink of water.

We haven't had much time since I got back to talk about what you've been doing, Ali, while I was away."

"Usual stuff," was her quick reply. "Tai chi, walking, spying, swimming, gaming, spying, shopping and, oh yes, spying," all stated in a monotone voice.

Dan laughed. "Usual stuff, then, as you say." He looked at Ali in such a way that she had to laugh too. They'd always had a similar sense of humour.

Very quickly, she outlined what had happened in his absence: her part in tracking down the criminals and the end result. She expanded the explanation to include how she'd worked with Super Techie on various aspects of coding and searching and the communications she'd had with Adrian Smythe. She also shared with Dan the fact that she was feeling at a bit of a loose end after her work with Adrian and his crew. At first, Dan didn't make any comment.

"Your job's not finished then, Ali, is it?" he finally commented.

"What do you mean?"

"Well, you've helped stop the bombs being placed and detonated this time, but what's happened to the rest of the castor beans? You've just told me that twenty-two tonnes had been bought, yet you've only recovered two bombs. The castor beans must be being stored somewhere, if they haven't already been made into bombs."

"You're right. Maybe I should contact Adrian to see if he still wants my help. Or Super Techie or…?"

Dan put his hand on Ali's arm.

"Breathe, Ali, breathe."

Ali went straight into a series of Qigong breath, feeling the calming effect almost immediately.

"You need to continue searching, monitoring and coding, if necessary. Adrian will still need your help. If other bombs have already been made, you need to help find out where they are now and where they're going to be planted. I'll help if I can but, really, these are your areas of expertise. I'm just a grunt this time." The last sentence said with a smile on his face.

"You'll never be just a grunt," Ali replied with feeling, "because you're adorable."

Dan's smile grew wider. "Of course I am, if you say so, but I'm sure others wouldn't agree."

"Who cares about others?" Ali said, as she leaned forward

17

to give Dan what she felt was a well-earned kiss.

***

Adrian Smythe had updated the whiteboard in his office. He had the names and locations of various players involved in the making, transporting and planting of the ricin bombs in Rosenbad, Sweden. He'd also listed the operatives who'd been involved in the operation. Adrian reflected on the quality of the people who'd been involved and came to the conclusion that he'd been very, very lucky to have people of such a high calibre. The end result could have been so much worse.

The persons in custody waiting to be interrogated were on one side of his board with their probable involvement in the last incident. Casualties were also listed. There was Said Ishak, the person who was to plant the bombs, who'd been attacked by Nessa Wakim when they'd been discovered in a house in Rosenbad with the bombs ready to be planted. He said he had been an innocent, who'd been fed lies and encouraged to plant the bombs because he'd been told he was chosen by the Prophet to do so; really? Adrian thought. Nessa Wakim, a well-known, vicious and vindictive terrorist, had attacked him when they'd been discovered. The blow to his head from her attack had left him unconscious and in hospital. Janie, one of the agents in the team in Rosenbad, had developed a reaction to the vaccine which would have protected her — as much as she could be protected — from the ricin in the bombs if they'd been detonated. She'd died before the agents had entered the house where the bombs were purported to be. Another agent, Evan, was in hospital after a less severe reaction and he seemed to be responding to treatment, but it was early days yet. The name Muttaqi Saladin was underlined. He had been the operative who'd alerted them to the fact that something significant was going to happen and that it could be catastrophic. He'd been undercover at the time but, since his last message, there'd been no sight of him. Going into the dragon's den was always a dangerous mission, but Muttaqi had been enthusiastic and hopeful. Was he still alive or was he, in fact, dead? That's the million-dollar question, thought Adrian, and he didn't believe he had the answer.

So deep in thought was Adrian that he hadn't registered the buzz on his laptop which was alerting him to the fact that the PM was ready and waiting to facetime with him.

"Here goes," he muttered under his breath.

"Good evening, Ma'am."

"Is it?" came the terse reply.

Chapter Two

Super Techie, real name Jo Jacobs, was totally immersed in the hardware that surrounded her and the software it held. For security reasons, Ali had not been given Jo's name when they'd started working together — the old 'need to know' chestnut, so Ali had made up the name Super Techie and Jo was happy to go with it. If truth be told, she quite liked it. Jo had worked very hard to get to such a senior position, particularly as she was a woman. In her industry, as in some others, it seemed to be men who usually got to the top. The software she'd written, tested and installed on various phones had been very successful for her. It made her voice sound rather masculine so people with whom she dealt just presumed that she was a man. She felt she got a better response to her work that way as males in some cultures were not happy working with women who were in a position of seniority. She believed it would be sinful not to use every talent you've got. She was happy to be Super Techie.

The Freedom for Fighters (FfF) website, which she had been scrutinising for days, was still getting traffic. Super Techie considered the various conversations and realised that the other players in the proposed bombing didn't seem to know that some of their people were in custody. As it was a black op, Adrian had kept everything out of the papers thus far, so it could be that there were more leads to be found to the people and the ricin. The only small news item had been in the Swedish press with a small piece on escaping gas and people having to be evacuated out of their houses in Rosenbad, Sweden. How he was keeping a lid on what really happened, Super Techie didn't know, but keeping a lid on it Adrian was!

"Hi, Super Techie, it's Ali. How are you doing?"

"You must be psychic, Ali. I was just going to ring you."

"Really?" answered Ali, rather flustered at hearing Super Techie's lovely voice again. The voice reminded Ali of an actor, but she couldn't quite bring the name to mind.

"Yes. I'm still monitoring the FfF website and I could do with a second opinion."

"On what?" replied Ali.

"Well, I don't want to influence you about what's on there. Would you go on the website and let me know what you find?"

No reply.

"If you're not happy to do that, Ali, don't worry about it. I thought you were in this with us?"

"It's just that I haven't heard anything from Adrian since, so not sure I'm still in the loop," stated Ali.

"I forgot you don't really know Adrian, Ali. Sorry. With Adrian, once you're in you're in. He makes it very plain when he doesn't want you in. Ergo, you've not heard, so you're still in! Sorry if I'm sounding a bit wired, but I've been drinking way too much coffee lately. I really need your very perceptive eyes just at this moment."

Ali went rather pink in the face, gave herself a quick shake and replied, "Happy to help. Will have a look and get back to you as soon as I can."

"That would be great. Think I need something more

substantial to eat before I start to hallucinate. I'm just going to take a short break then I'll be back at my desk."

"Good advice. Just having some Jasmine tea and a bite of lunch myself, then I'll get straight on it. Speak with you soon."

"You okay?" Dan asked as she entered the kitchen. "Your face looks a bit flushed."

Ali laughed self-consciously. "I'm fine," she replied, as Dan continued to stare at her.

"I've just been chatting to Super Techie and he still wants my help. I said I'd have a bite of lunch and then look at the FfF website I told you about."

"Okay. Are you doing that here or at his place?" Dan asked, still staring at her.

"Here. Always here. I don't know where his place is!"

"Ummm." Then, after a few seconds, "I'm popping to the gun shop as I need more cartridges. I used quite a lot on my last trip. Let me know if there's anything I can do to help when I get back."

"I will. Thanks."

Dan leant into her, gave her a hug and a lingering kiss.

"Remember, I love you," he said, gazing into her eyes, "and I'll be back."

"Okay," was all she could manage. What was all that about, lovely though it was? Dan was always loving, but that was something else. If that's how he is when he comes home from a trip, maybe he needs to go away more! She giggled quietly to herself as she went off to eat the falafel salad, she'd left in the fridge the previous day.

Dan had other thoughts on his mind. He did need more cartridges, but he also needed some time to himself to think. Was something more going on with Ali and Super Techie? He knew Ali loved him, but was he going away too much and leaving her open to comfort from elsewhere? He couldn't believe that. He wouldn't believe it, but maybe he shouldn't go away for a while. Life can be very complicated, thought Dan, and he really didn't like complicated!

***

At the Zakaria Masjd Mosque in Chapel Street, Leeds, men hurried to their prayers. Some friends were exchanging a few words before they entered; others were heads down already contemplating the forthcoming prayer time. Close by, Maura Grainger was sitting in her car pretending to read a magazine. She was a member of the team who'd been observing the mosque for some time as there were concerns about radicalisation of young men who attended. She'd also been part of the pursuit team who'd followed Said Ishak, a prospective bomber, into London before he boarded a train on his journey to Sweden. Although some members of the mosque who'd also been involved had been arrested, it wasn't sure whether all were in the bag. This meant that surveillance had to continue.

It wasn't obvious that this is what Maura was doing as she was sitting in a car with medical emergency emblems on the outside. It was standard practice for these cars to be situated in various places, rather than always at a depot, because if there was an accident or incident, cars could come from all directions, rather than being kept in one place. As long as she moved at least once in the day, and left at 8 pm at the latest, locals would believe she was legitimate and was returning to the depot for the evening. Jim Adams, another member of the team, was in an alley, keeping watch. The third member of the team, Shihab Ozer, was off sick as he'd been injured whilst pursuing the car transporting Said Ishak to his destination — St Pancras train station. He'd been replaced temporarily by Mike Jones, who was currently in their shared accommodation, trying to catch some sleep before their shift changes.

Jim stretched his legs and tried not to breathe in as the stench of urine in the alley was very strong. Two more hours and he would be going back to the house for some sleep, changing his location with Mike. He couldn't wait as nothing seemed to be happening at the Zakaria Masjd Mosque. Mike was good, but Jim missed Shihab and his dry sense of humour. Hopefully, it won't be too long before he's back, he reflected, as he knew that they were a stronger team when they were working together.

Inside the mosque, Mustafa Younan was totally engrossed in his prayers. He had begun work on the three bombs and had come to the mosque to see if Abdul-Azeem Tawfeek would be there. Mustafa knew that he had been chosen to use his skills to do the work for the Prophet and he was happy to do that. He did wonder why Tawfeek wasn't at the mosque but, after thinking about it for a short time, decided that this was obviously a test set for him by Tawfeek. He wouldn't fail him. As he'd been instructed, Mustafa hadn't told anyone about his bombmaking activities so he was feeling a bit isolated. He would have liked to discuss with someone how to proceed if Tawfeek didn't show up when the bombs were to be collected, but then he decided that he was looking for problems where there were none. Of course, this was a test. He wouldn't fail. Mustafa threw himself into his prayers with renewed vigour.

The beautiful prayers from the Qur'an lifted his spirits and made him feel closer to the Prophet. Had Mustafa known that Tawfeek was currently locked away and being questioned about a prospective bombing in Rosenbad, Sweden, perhaps he wouldn't have been so enthusiastic?

Chapter Three

Jenny Evans was looking through the agenda for her programme later that evening. "The usual items," she mused, and a short interview with a CEO from Winning Ways Academy Trust. That could be an interesting one as there was mixed feelings about these trusts with them often seen as part of hostile takeovers of schools. It could get interesting.

"Welcome to South East Today where we bring you up-to-date news and interviews on some issues which are high profile," stated Jenny, as she stared into the front camera.

"Today, we have with us, Edward Johnson, the CEO of the Winning Ways Academy Trust. Welcome, Mr Johnson, and thank you for taking the time out of your busy schedule to be here today."

"My pleasure," came the stock reply.

"There have been some concerns lately about the almost exponential growth of academies in education…" stated Jenny, not able to finish before she was interrupted.

"Concerns? By whom?"

Momentarily taken aback, Jenny quickly recovered her poise.

"Concerns of parents of some of the children in the schools within the Trust."

"We have a policy for complaints. Any parent can access it on the website of each school. Once a complaint is received, it's dealt with according to the policy."

This is like talking to a robot, Jenny was thinking. No change in tone of voice or facial expression; arrogance or disinterest?

"I think you're missing the point, Mr Johnson. I'm not asking about complaints per se, but about concerns that some parents have. In the push to improve outcomes, is the welfare of the children and, in some cases the teachers, being overlooked or ignored?"

"The Trust delivers a strong and successful improvement service. It supports schools to enable success for the children. How can there be a complaint about that?" Mr Johnson asked.

"It is how it delivers, that is the concern. I'm talking about the pastoral side of education in which children can celebrate their successes, discover and develop new talents with teachers who also feel valued and supported. Some parents have stated that is not happening. In fact, they believe any child not achieving academic success is overlooked or ignored."

"Rubbish. Our results speak for themselves," came the tart reply. "We also supply enrichment activities: science workshops and trips away are just some of things we do. Quite soon, some children from one of our schools are going on a trip to Dunkirk and then onto Cologne. They'll visit battlefields from World War II and various places of interest then, after a couple of days, travel onwards to explore Cologne. They're just some of the opportunities we provide for the children."

"That's commendable and I'm sure the children will have a great time."

"Yes, they will."

Almost sounds like a command, Jenny thought.

"Going back to the first concerns, though academic results do seem to improve when the Trust takes over, when you take into account the number of permanent exclusions, aren't you just moving children on who have proved to be problematic so that your results aren't adversely affected?"

"No."

"What about when the Trust takes over schools. The turnover of staff is substantially above the norm for at least a year afterwards. Can you explain that?"

"The Trust delivers a strong and successful improvement service. It supports schools to enable success for the children. To do that, we have to ensure we have the best teachers."

Jenny realised that Edward Johnson had his stock answers and she wouldn't budge him, so she tried another tack.

"Your Trust must be approaching about twenty schools now? Do you think there should be a limit to the number of schools in a trust?"

"As long as a trust can continue to make improvements, it should be allowed to add to its number of schools," swiftly replied.

"How then can the administration within the Trust manage the constant changes? In your case, as we recently read in the press, your salary is now in the region of £160,000, yet the terms and conditions of the teachers within the Trust don't seem to have changed at all."

"I'm not here to discuss the administration within the Trust or a possible salary for myself. All I will say is people within the Trust are paid according to their ability and the position they hold."

"Do you believe that your role as CEO of a Trust merits a substantially higher salary than someone, such as our Prime

Minister, who is responsible for the well-being of the country?"

"The two positions are not comparable."

It was time to draw the interview to a close and Jenny couldn't have been more pleased.

"What would you say to the people who've voiced concerns about the running of schools in the Trust?"

"The Trust delivers a strong and successful improvement service. It supports schools to enable success for the children. It is the way forward for education."

"Thank you, again, Mr Johnson."

The camera flashes back to the news desk where Jenny continues with the current news.

Sitting in their terraced house in Teynham, Kent, Dilawar Lodi and his dad, Qusay, had watched the interview on South East Today.

"Edward Johnson, isn't he something to do with your school?" Qusay asked his son.

"We see him in school sometimes talking to Mrs Williams, our Headteacher, but I don't really know what his job is. I don't like him very much though," replied Dilawar.

"Why? He was a bit stiff on the telly, but he seemed to know about your trip?" his dad stated.

"I don't think he's respectful to the lady teachers; the young ones any way."

"What do you mean, not respectful? Have you ever seen him do anything wrong?" real concern in his dad's voice now.

"Nooooo. It's just, he seems to be staring at them all the time, watching them as they walk away. It doesn't seem respectful to me, especially as some of the teachers aren't much older than me really. It feels a bit creepy," he replied hestitantly.

"Ahh, Dilawar, you listen too much to your grandpa. Men like to look at women; it doesn't mean they're doing anything wrong."

Dilawar didn't reply. He hated it when his dad spoke about Jadd like that. Jadd believed in the Prophet and went to the mosque regularly to pray. He was a well-known and liked Imam too, who made sure he prayed five times a day as he should. Dad didn't go to the mosque very much and certainly didn't pray as often as he should. Too westernised, Jadd would say; perhaps he was right. Dilawar had seen how some of the boys and girls behaved at school and he was disturbed by it. Jadd had told him that women were to be respected and were to keep themselves pure until marriage. From what Dilawar had seen that wasn't what was happening. Some of the behaviours he'd witnessed at school and on TV were as far from pure as you could get. It confused and upset him.

Qusay took his son's silence as acceptance of what he'd said. In the future, would Qusay remember the adage, 'don't take silence for agreement'?

"Just a few days until you go up to Leeds to visit your grandpa and, when you come back, it will only be a couple of days until you go on your trip. I'll bet it'll be an eventful trip."

It will be eventful alright, thought Dilawar. It will be explosive!

***

Ten minutes after the programme finished, Jenny Evans was still at her desk sorting out her paperwork.

"Well, you had a right bright spark on tonight, Jenny. He

30

couldn't be any more wooden if he'd had a stick up his bum."

Jenny laughed. Gwen Masters, her colleague, never lost her temper and never swore so anything detrimental she said about anyone had an almost childlike quality. "Is he always so charismatic?"

"I'm led to believe he's very charismatic with the ladies, if you know what I mean?"

"Really? I suppose he wasn't bad looking. Piercing green eyes and reasonable features, but he really did have a wobbly mouth."

Jenny almost choked trying to contain her laughter.

"What do you mean, 'wobbly mouth'?"

"His lips are floppy. That's the best I can do to explain it."

"I think I know what you mean." Again, Jenny stifled a laugh. "You'd think he'd have better dress sense if he's making all that money and is such high profile in the Trust."

"He must be very clever then. How many times have we seen it, though, extremely clever and zilch social skills?" asked Gwen.

"He can't be that clever," replied Jenny.

"Okay, dish the dirt."

When they were setting up the Trust, he wanted to call it The Winners' Academy Trust."

"And?"

Jenny wrote the proposed name and then, in brackets, the initials by which it would be known.

Gwen watched as she wrote the initials and burst out laughing herself.

"Oh dear! Did someone enlighten Mr Wooden before it was all made legal?"

"Obviously, or he'd be one from one!"

There was raucous laughter for a few minutes, then sighs, as they both composed themselves.

"Time for a quick coffee and then home," Jenny commented, as they both left the studio.

"Sounds good to me," stated Gwen in reply.

Chapter Four

Ali finished her lunch, stood up and stretched. Having no tai chi lessons planned for the next few weeks was beginning to tell on her equilibrium. She knew her instructors needed to have their holidays, but she did miss the sessions. Doing some moves at home was an option, but Ali didn't feel she got the same out of it as when she did it in a class. Standing like a tree, on your own, just looked a bit silly. Qigong breaths were okay, but Ali missed doing the 8, 16, 24 or 40 moves with the rest of the class. Focussing on those moves helped to keep her calm and relaxed. Ali also missed popping into Costa Coffee afterwards with her friends, chatting and sharing experiences. However, she knew she couldn't share her spying activities with them, which did make her a little anxious in case she slipped up.

"Okay," Ali whispered to herself. "Get a grip."

She walked to her computer, sparked it up and logged on. A very quick check of her emails to see if there was anything that needed to be dealt with urgently — there wasn't — then onto the Dark Web. First job was inputting the software she'd written to protect her identity on that extremely dark network. Ali had been aghast when she'd first gone on the Dark Web, curious to see what was on offer there. What a shock to find the services included guns, illegal drugs, counterfeiters, some very nasty porn, violence for hire and even some suggestion of human trafficking; plus, a whole lot more of what Ali felt was pure evil. Inputting additional software, before going on the web and different software just before she came off, offered her peace of mind that her IP address couldn't be traced back to her. She logged in as pi235711 on the Freedom for Fighters (FfF) website, scanning the messages on there. The messages were from the people who were involved in the proposed bombing in Sweden and Ali had the code to decipher them. Super Techie and James, her colleague, had managed to break the code so that all the messages could be captured.

After about two hours, Ali logged out of the FfF website and then sat back on her chair and surveyed the notes she'd made. She began to extract information from the notes, compiling various lists. Ali knew some of the original participants were currently in custody because Adrian had told her. Another list had the names of people using the code whose identity she didn't know and the final list seemed to be people who actually wanted to fight for some right or other. One name wanted to marry a horse, another wanted to have relationship with a zombie. At this point, Ali decided that enough was enough. She ran the exit software and then logged off the computer.

The phone was picked up at the third ring.

"Hi Super Techie; it's Ali."

"I know; I've got number recognition on my phone."

"Of course, you have," replied Ali.

"Did you look on the FfF website?"

"I did."

"And?"

"And, I don't think they know we've got some people in custody. The messages are a continuation of what they were discussing before. Well, not quite the same."

"What do you mean?" asked Super Techie.

"The names are not the same. There's the odd couple that were on before, but whom we haven't been able to trace, and there's also a couple of other people too. It feels like something else is going to happen. I can't quite explain it," stated Ali.

"That's exactly what I felt," replied Super Techie. I just can't quite put my finger on what it is. I told you I needed your eyes and a second opinion. I wasn't wrong, was I?"

"No, you weren't wrong. We're obviously both on the same wavelength, which is good."

"Better than good, I think."

Ali flushed. What was it with the phone and Super Techie?

"I'll do what I can and get back to you. Okay?"

"More than okay, Ali; thank you. I look forward to hearing from you again soon."

"Me too," Ali replied.

"Who was that on the phone?" asked Dan, as he walked into the room.

Ali gave a start as she hadn't heard him come in.

"It was Super Techie. It seems we're both on the same wavelength with the FfF website, so I'm going to keep scanning the messages and see what, if anything, I can pick up."

"Oh. Sounds like a good plan," Dan replied.

If Ali caught the note of insincerity in his voice, she didn't comment on it.

"Did you get everything you needed at the gun shop?"

"More or less." he replied.

Are you going away again so soon?" Ali asked.

"Probably not; I've got a few things to catch up on here."

"It'll be good to have you around for a while."

"Yes, won't it?" Dan said as he watched Ali walk off into the kitchen.

***

In the office of Specialised Security Systems in Great Smith Street, Adrian Smythe stood, hands in pockets, looking at the whiteboard. He had added to the information and was now surveying the results.

Said Ishak, the proposed bomber in Sweden, had been put into an induced coma in hospital to try to stabilise his condition. He was now in a locked ward under close observation. The swelling around his brain seemed to be growing and putting him into an agitated state. It was hoped the coma would give Ishak at least a chance of a recovery. Adrian wasn't optimistic about his chances. He wondered, as he gazed at the whiteboard, if they would ever truly know how Ishak had become involved. The Zakaria Masjd Mosque played a central part in all that had happened, Adrian was sure, but finding enough evidence to support what he thought was proving difficult.

Nessa Wakim would give them nothing. Zealots seldom did. She had been put into isolation in prison in Sweden, as much for the safety of the other inmates as for her own. Her vicious nature and violent temper would be attractive to some of the weaker elements in the prison. Attempts had been, and would continue to be made, to try to get information from her, but Adrian wasn't hopeful that they would be successful.

Meena Wakim, Nessa's daughter, was in custody too. They didn't really know what to do with her as she had been made to go with her mother and had been both physically and verbally abused by her. She had, however, been prepared to go out with Ishak and plant the bombs; even though she wasn't aware they contained ricin. Being weak and subservient wasn't acceptable as an excuse for killing people; she did know they were bombs. Meena had been questioned and she had told them as much as she knew, but that wasn't much at all.

***

Abdul-Aalee Khatib sat in his cell, gazing at the bare walls and wondering how the police had been able to arrest him. He was going over in his head, the events leading up to his arrest. Khatib couldn't think how the police had known about his involvement. Had he been betrayed, he wondered?

"Who? Who could it be?" he whispered under his breath.

Stroking his forehead, as he did when he was deep in thought, he tried to make a mental list of anyone who could benefit from his arrest. So great was his arrogance that he couldn't think of anyone. He did fleetingly consider Abdul-Azeem Tawfeek, but could see no benefit for him if they were caught. Khatib knew that Tawfeek believed in their mission and enjoyed the active engagement, so he dismissed the idea of his being a traitor. No one had spoken to him since he was put in the cell. With righteous indignation, he had demanded a solicitor, threatening all sorts of ills on the police, the government, anyone he could think of. He became silent when he was told that he was being held under the Terrorism Act 2000 and someone would talk to him in due course. Did this mean they knew about the bombs, he wondered? He hadn't heard anything about bombs going off in Sweden, but then he hadn't had any contact with anyone since he was arrested. Khatib could feel his anger mounting. He tried to pray, but the beautiful words from the Qur'an didn't seem to touch him, or give him any comfort. Perhaps his twisting of their meaning to get others to do his bidding had made it difficult for him to pray with any sincerity. He tried to work out what the authorities knew and what they could find out about his involvement with the bombs, so that when someone did come to talk with him, he would be ready.

In another cell in the same building, Abdul-Azeem Tawfeek wondered if Mustafa Younan had begun making the new bombs as he'd been instructed or if he'd been arrested too. Tawfeek wondered if Mustafa, with his loose tongue, had led to his arrest. If it was him, Tawfeek would deal with him when he was released. Tawfeek, too, tried to pray, but his anger would not allow him to focus on the prayers he led so often in the mosque. He did believe in the Prophet and all his teachings, but he also believed that his interpretations were the correct ones, not realising how he was debasing those same teachings by his actions. No one had been in to speak with Tawfeek and although he had banged on the door of his cell, shouted and screamed in anger; no one came. In some ways, he found this more unsettling. He was used to manipulating people to do his will and, he knew, making them fearful not to do so. How could he be kept in a cell without conversations being held or deals being made?

***

Evan Olsen, the Swedish agent who'd had an adverse reaction to the anti-ricin vaccine RTA $1 - 33/44 - 198$, was making good progress. He was having lots of blood samples taken and they were rushed to Porton Down to see if there was anything in the blood which would help to improve the vaccine. The scientists there were hopeful, but did not have anything useful yet. The funeral of Janie Larsen had been arranged and a quiet ceremony would take place the following week. Blood samples had been taken from her, too, just after she had been vaccinated. Again, they were sent post haste to Porton Down, where they were making as much vaccine as they could in case other bombs were discovered in the near future. The problem with the vaccine was that it was a fragment of the ricin A-chain that had been modified to get rid of the toxic enzymatic property of RTA, increase its stability and maintain its ability to produce a protective immune response. However, there are sometimes allergic reactions and some longer lasting side effects. Any samples taken after vaccination could help to identify reasons for the adverse effects as testing on anything living, whether animal or human, had been impossible before. In this case, being vaccinated had been the only safeguard for the team members who were to enter the house where the bombs were thought to be kept.

Shihab Ozer who been involved in a biking accident while following the bomber, Said Ishak, was improving quickly and hoping to be back with his team observing the area around the Zakaria Masjd Mosque. As a Muslim himself, he dreaded the thought that death and destruction could be caused yet again in the name of Islam if ricin bombs were set off. Not on my watch, he thought, because he knew that the repercussions for the majority of Muslims would be devastating, despite the fact that most of them were peaceful and just wanted to live their lives.

Nothing more had been heard about Muttaqi Saladin. Had he been radicalised? Was he dead?

Chapter Five

Dilawar Lodi settled into his seat on the National Express coach which would take him from Victoria Coach Station in London to Leeds. His dad wanted to drive him up to Leeds to see his grandad but, being fifteen years of age, Dilawar refused to be chauffeured. He was happy for his dad to put him on the train to London Victoria and he only had to walk around the corner at Victoria to get to the coach station. He was hoping that the traffic wouldn't be too bad so that the journey would only take about four hours. He hated the stops at the services because everyone would rush into the building to get into the toilets, and then rush around trying to get a hot drink to take back onto the coach. At one time, you could get a hot drink on the coach, but not anymore. If you had a hot drink, you might burn yourself! How stupid many of those health and safety rules were as they took away any common-sense people might have. If you didn't know that a hot drink might burn you if it dropped on you, you shouldn't be out on your own. Dilawar put his headphones on, closed his eyes and settled back to listen to his music, hoping that he could get some sleep en route.

***

Mashuum Lodi, Dilawar's grandad, was preparing the bedroom for his grandson. He wished they lived nearer to him so he could take Dilawar to the mosque where they could pray together. Mashuum was an Imam, so he was high profile in the mosque. His son, Qusay, didn't keep to his religion and Mashuum felt the Prophet must be very sad about that. He also felt that it reflected badly on him, but Qusay couldn't see that at all. Qusay had married a non-Muslim woman two years after his wife had died and, although she was a kind woman who seemed to care for Qusay and Dilawar, she didn't understand how important Islam was to them all; or how important it should have been. Dilawar was choosing to go to the mosque when he went up to Leeds and Mashuum was very happy about that. When Dilawar was born, his name was chosen because it meant brave and courageous. Mashuum hoped he would be both of those things.

***

Waking with a start, it took Dilawar a few seconds to orientate himself. Rubbing his eyes, he could see they had just stopped in the services and people were jostling to get off the bus. Surely no one wants the toilet that badly? he thought. Dilawar waited until the aisle was almost clear to stand up and work his way to the front of the coach.

"Back in twenty minutes," stated the driver as he stepped down from the coach.

"Okay."

Dilawar walked past a group of young men who were waiting in line at one of the stands. He could hear them giggling as he passed, but he paid them no heed, walking towards the toilet area. Although there was a longish queue for the ladies' toilet, Dilawar was able to walk straight into the men's. He was soon washing his hands and walking back towards the coach. Out of the corner of his eye, he could see the young men he'd seen earlier pushing each other and laughing. He was almost past them when one of them shouted something to him. He continued walking, but had to stop suddenly when one of them walked directly in front of him, facing him.

"Didn't you hear me shout at you?" the tall youth asked, staring right in his face.

"Didn't realise you were shouting me," Dilawar replied, refusing to break the stare.

The two stood facing each other for what felt like a lifetime to Dilawar, but was only a few seconds.

The youth's face split into a large smile as he produced something from behind his back.

"I thought you looked hungry when you passed us the first time, so I bought you a bacon sandwich."

Dilawar's expression didn't change, but his eyes became dark with anger. He stepped to his right and carried on walking towards the coach, not uttering a word. It wasn't the reaction that the youths had expected so they were silent for a minute.

"He must be a pig hater," one of them said, "but if you look at their women, that can't be true."

They all laughed then carried on pushing each other and laughing.

Dilawar could feel his face flush red, burning with embarrassment but also with such a deep anger, he could almost taste it.

Why, why, why? He asked himself. What did I ever do to

them that they insult me and all Muslim women? What can I do about it? At that moment, he had no answers. But, soon, he would have.

When he got back on the coach, Dilawar couldn't settle at all. His music didn't engage him and he didn't bring anything to read, so he was wondering how he could pass the time until the end of his journey. There was no one in the seat next to him so he took some time to look at others on the coach and decided to listen in to their conversations if he could. In the seat in front of his was what looked like a grandmother and her granddaughter.

"Would you like a sandwich, Elle?"

"No."

"Some fruit?

"No."

"How about a nice biscuit?"

"No."

"Some chocolate?"

"No."

"What would you like then?" asked the woman in exasperation.

There was a slight pause before Elle replied, "I want to go home. I don't want to go on this trip with you."

"Oh, Elle," hurt in her voice now. "You've no choice, I'm sorry. Your aunt and uncle are going to look after you until your mum gets better."

"Oh, yeah. Gets better, that's a laugh! You don't get better from drugs, do you?"

"Well, we'll see," came the swift reply.

Elle grunted and turned her head back towards the window. She couldn't be more than ten years old, how could

43

her mum not want to look after her? Dilawar thought of his own mum and how well she'd looked after him and loved him. He remembered her death and how alone he'd felt. He hadn't been happy when, after a year, his dad started to go out again, or when he'd introduced him to Anna, his girlfriend. Dilawar didn't want his mum replaced. Anyway, Anna didn't try to take his mum's place and she was always kind and thoughtful to him so, when his dad married her, Dilawar was pleased for his dad. She still didn't try to take his mum's place and Dilawar could see she loved his dad, so he was okay with the relationship. He just wished she'd been a Muslim and then, perhaps, his dad would have kept going to the mosque. He'd pray to the Prophet for his dad when he went to the mosque with his grandad.

"Don't, I'm not like that," a voice whispered across the aisle.

In that seat was a young girl sitting by the window and a young boy next to her. Both looked about the same age as Dilawar, but the girl could have been younger.

The boy looked very annoyed.

"I just touched your back when I kissed you, that's all," he replied.

"You moved it inside my jumper and tried to undo my bra. I'm not like that."

The boy let out a grunt.

"I thought you were my girlfriend?"

"I am your girlfriend."

"You wouldn't think so, the way you behave. It's like you don't want me to touch you at all. How can I kiss you if I can't touch you?"

The girl stared into the boy's face, seeing hurt and upset.

"I… I… Well, of course you can't kiss me if you can't touch me. Just don't go inside my clothes."

"Okay," whispered the boy, pulling her close to him, kissing her and putting his hand just inside the bottom of her jumper.

The girl didn't seem to notice. The kiss ended and the girl turned to look out of the window. The boy noticed Dilawar watching and smiled, winking at him as his smile widened and giving Dilawar a thumbs up.

Where is the respect there? Dilawar turned away and decided that he didn't want to see or hear any more; he would listen to his music and, hopefully, drift off to sleep. He must have slept eventually and, when he woke up about an hour or so later, in the seat to his right, the girl was leaning with her back against the boy's chest. Her eyes were closed and Dilawar was sure that the boy had his hand inside the front of her jumper, rubbing her breasts. Sensing him looking, the boy twisted his head around and winked at Dilawar again. No respect here at all.

As they came into Leeds Coach Station, in Wellington Street, Dilawar could see his grandad standing by the bench at the side. The coach pulled in and everyone got off, going to the side compartment where the driver was dragging cases out and putting them on the floor for people to collect. Dilawar waited until his bag was removed and then made his way over to his grandad, who smiled with pleasure to see him.

"Jadd," Dilawar said, as his grandad wrapped him in strong arms. "I can't tell you how happy I am to be here. I mean, I really can't tell you."

"It's good to see you too, Dilawar, my brave and courageous one."

They hurried out of the station, glad to be going home together.

45

Chapter Six

Dilawar was up early the next morning, keen to pray with his grandad. He loved the prayers of the Qur'an as they filled him with a sort of peace inside. The stories about how the prayers were given to the Prophet were ones with which he was becoming familiar. In some ways, the fact that the Prophet couldn't read, but had to learn the prayers by rote from the Archangel, gave him comfort. Dilawar wasn't a great scholar either, but he did enjoy reading and, unlike a lot of his contemporaries, he loved poetry. To him, the prayers were poetic, yet still relevant. When he glanced at his grandad's face as he was praying, it reminded him of something he'd read at school. His grandad's face seemed to be filled with an inner light similar to what he thought Jesus Christ's face was said to look like when he was transfigured on the mountain. In the religion of Islam, Jesus was recognised as a prophet; not the saviour, though, that the Christians believed.

After prayers, Dilawar and his grandad sat down to quite a large breakfast, catching up on each other's news.

"Jadd, why do some people hate us so, when they don't even know us?" Dilawar asked.

"They're ignorant, usually, and we're the scapegoat for all their ills."

Dilawar didn't really understand what that meant, but he continued, "Why did the boys at the services taunt me with a bacon sandwich, when they know we don't eat pork?"

"Again, Dilawar, they're ignorant. They probably thought you'd react in a different way, so they could make fun of you. Perhaps they thought you'd be weak. I'm proud that you walked away. You can't win with that type of person."

"I realise that, Jadd, but I can't understand why they would want to do it. They don't even know me. I was so angry, especially when they said those things about our women."

"I know you don't think it, Dilawar, but you did the right thing. Perhaps next time they see a Muslim boy, they'll leave him alone because they think he'll react as you did. If they don't get a reaction, they will move on to something else."

"Or someone else?"

"Perhaps," he answered. "We can't save the world; we can only live in the best way possible."

Dilawar didn't agree with his grandad, but he didn't say anything.

Once they'd had breakfast, Dilawar went on Snapchat to send a message to his friend, Zaigham, letting him know he'd arrived at his grandad's, but would be back in time for the school trip. He attached a funny picture, secure in the knowledge that once Zaigham had read the message, it would be deleted as he was the only recipient. What Dilawar didn't know was that his dad, Qusay, had put mSpy software onto Dilawar's phone so he got to see every message Dilawar sent. Qusay felt that was a very good way to keep track of what Dilawar was up to and who his friends were. When Qusay was alerted that Dilawar had sent a Snapchat message to someone, he glanced at it, smiled to himself at the picture and deleted it.

"Dilawar, it's time to go to the mosque. Are you ready?"

"Yes, Jadd, I'm coming now."

Mashuum double-locked the front door of the house as they left and, together, they set off for the Zakaria Masjd Mosque, chatting about everything and nothing as they walked. After about fifteen minutes, they were walking up the steps to the mosque, ready to pray with the others within. Sitting in her car close to the mosque, Maura Grainger lifted her phone and took a couple of snaps of them. Since the attempted bombing in Sweden, and subsequent arrest of some of the members of the mosque, the team had been instructed to take photos of anyone entering and leaving. These were sent to Alan Edwards, the chief of the Leeds office, to peruse and forward as required. A new face was always interesting and one so young with an older man, more so. Maura wondered what the relationship was between the two who were talking so animatedly. Were they Father and son, grandad and grandson or uncle and nephew? Looking at the picture, Maura could see a strong facial resemblance so she thought father and son, or grandad and grandson, were the most probable. Hard to tell sometimes because often older men married quite young girls so the children could be their children rather than grandchildren.

***

In his office in Leeds, Alan Edwards looked at the recent pictures and decided that it was best to forward them to Adrian Smythe for his team to collate. At the end of the day, they had the resources to look for matches to anyone who was known to have militant tendencies. In fact, one piece of software Jo Jacobs had written was excellent for facial recognition and also for finding familial similarities. If they couldn't find a match with that, there probably wasn't one.

***

At that precise moment, Jo Jacobs — Super Techie — was sifting through messages being sent on the FfF website. She was making a list of contributors to that site too. A list she would compare to the list on which Ali Andrews was working. It could be quite difficult to root out the clientele who did really want freedom to do what they liked, against those who wanted to make violent statements — as in bombs — as some were using nicknames and sometimes the messages made little sense. They used the code to decipher them, but they were sometimes left with messages like: 'The bird has not yet sailed or the package is not wrapped yet.' What the hell was that supposed to mean? Jo ran her hands through her hair, sighed loudly and then went back to the site. She knew, just knew, that something was going to happen. You could call it a sixth sense but, whatever it was, she could also feel that the time scale for whatever was to happen was relatively soon, but how soon is relatively soon? she was thinking

"Hi, Ali, got anything to share?"

"I think I might have," she replied.

"That would be great."

"Some of the messages are what you'd expect on such a site: deviation, sexual gratification, abnormal desires and the like," Ali replied, feeling very uncomfortable and a bit pink in the face. "But some of the others are, I believe, talking about things relating to a bomb or bombs."

"How so?"

"Do you find the phrase about the package not being wrapped yet?"

"Yes, I did."

"Do you think that could mean that the bomb isn't ready yet; that it's still being made?"

A pregnant pause, then Super Techie replied," It could be I suppose, but it's a bit of a stretch don't you think? We would have to have a bit more than that."

"It was just a thought," replied Ali, feeling a bit foolish to have made such a huge leap with so little evidence.

"Hey, don't worry about it. Sometimes what we believe is correct, but we've got to find the evidence to substantiate it. 'Always trust your gut,' is what Adrian says and he's usually right. Keep at it, Ali. At least you seem to be getting somewhere while I'm struggling to see any meaning in anything."

"It's always darkest before dawn?" volunteered Ali, with some humour.

Super Techie laughed. Not really sure what that meant either, but it does seem to fit. "It's always good to talk with you, Ali, speak later."

"Always good to talk with you, too," Ali replied.

Ali jumped as she heard Dan's voice. She hadn't realised he'd come into the room. "Super Techie again?"

"Yes. We're just sharing our findings; although, we've not got much to share at the moment."

"I don't know; you seemed to have quite a bit to share."

Ali had no reply for this and was somewhat bemused by Dan's comment. Before she could say anything else, Dan had left the room.

Strange!

Chapter Seven

Dilawar was lost in prayer, letting the words from the Qur'an flow through him. He could feel the power of the prayers and was energised by it. How could his dad walk away from this? Dilawar couldn't remember the last time his dad had attended a mosque. He felt sure his grandad was hurt by his dad's casual approach to his religion; particularly, as he, as Imam, was such a leading force. Who can understand parents?

As Dilawar got to his feet, he could feel eyes staring at him. Looking to his left, he saw a man he'd spoken to on quite a few occasions when he'd been in the mosque, looking his way. The man waved. Dilawar was trying really hard to remember what he was called as the man walked towards him. Mustafa, that was it, he thought, relief in his face.

"As-salāmu alaykum," said Mustafa.

"Wa alaykumu s-salām," replied Dilawar.

The usual Muslim greeting for males, wishing each other peace; what better place to wish that than in a mosque?

"Are you going in the back room later?" Mustafa asked.

"I thought I might. Abdul-Azeem Tawfeek speaks with such fire," replied Dilawar, his face animated with pleasure.

"It isn't him today. I think he's away somewhere and not sure when he'll be back," stated Mustafa.

"Oh, but… Oh," stammered Dilawar, his face contorted as if he was in pain.

"Are you okay?" asked Mustafa, aware that something was wrong.

"No, it's okay. I just… erm… He was going to… Never mind, it's okay."

Mustafa was now even surer something was wrong. Knowing Tawfeek, Mustafa wondered if Dilawar's obvious distress was something to do with the bombs he was making.

"How long are you here for?" Mustafa asked.

"Got four more days until I return home," said Dilawar in reply.

"I'm sure he'll be back before then, so don't worry."

"Yes, you're right. Thank you."

Mustafa walked with Dilawar into the back room where Mashuum Lodi, Dilawar's grandfather, was to be the speaker. They both settled into position on the floor and turned towards Mashuum at the front. Dilawar found it hard to concentrate as Tawfeek's absence had disturbed him. How could he do what he had to do if Tawfeek wasn't there to instruct him? He tried to put his anxious thoughts away so he could concentrate on what his grandfather was saying. If you had been looking at Mustafa, you would have thought he was fully engaged in thinking about what the preacher was saying but, in fact, he was casting furtive glances at Dilawar. Mustafa could see that Tawfeek's absence had rattled Dilawar and he thought that it could be something to do with the bombs. He decided to befriend Dilawar and see if he could find out more about him and, perhaps, see if he was part of Tawfeek's plan for the other bombs.

After the talk, Mustafa and Dilawar walked out of the room together.

"Why don't you come into the room over there?" Mustafa

asked, pointing to a small door at the back of the mosque. "It's where we sit to socialise and solve the problems of the world?"

Dilawar laughed. "That would take more than the four days I've got left at my grandfather's," he replied, "but it would be good to talk to someone about things other than the Qur'an and my grandfather's got a bit to do here before we can go home."

They both chuckled as they walked towards the room. When they went in there was no one else there so they had the choice of seating and location. Mustafa steered Dilawar to two rather large armchairs by the windows while he got two cups of water out of the large water bottle nearby.

Soon, they were chatting like old friends. Well, Dilawar, who was usually quite shy, was talking as if he'd known Mustafa all his life. Telling how he didn't like school because of some of the behaviour of some of the children — boys and girls — who were disrespectful to each other and, sometimes, to themselves. Dilawar told Mustafa about his journey and about how angry he was about what had happened in the services and what he'd seen and heard on the coach.

"They have no respect, Dilawar," added Mustafa. "They hate us, yet they don't know us."

"Yes! Thank you! That's just what I said to my grandfather, but he said they were ignorant and I should ignore them."

"Ahhh, yes, but sometimes we have to stand up and be men. Not let Islam be abused or insulted, so these ignorant people do begin to know who we are and begin to fear us!" replied Mustafa, his face coloured by anger.

"Fear us?" questioned Dilawar, sounding unsure.

"What good did it do to their Jesus Christ to be forgiving

53

and turning the other cheek? They thought he was a saviour, but he died a horrible death on the cross, like a thief. When you're weak or you pander to the bully, all you get is pain and more pain. If you are strong, they fear you and fear is power. Can't you see that?"

Dilawar didn't speak for a few minutes, his face a picture of uncertainty and indecision. "Yes, I can see that. I can."

"Dilawar, there you are," stated Mashuum as he popped his head around the door into the room in which the two young men were sitting. "I'll be ready to go in about fifteen minutes. That okay with you?"

"Of course, Jadd, I'll be ready."

For a minute after Mashuum left, there was complete silence.

"Are you coming tomorrow?" asked Mustafa, a germ of an idea forming in his brain.

"Yes, I'll be here every day for the next three days. Why?"

"It's been good to talk to you and I would like to talk more. It's not often we get younger men like you in our mosque who can share what's happening in their world. I thought I'd take advantage of such a good opportunity."

"That's great, thanks. You must be one of the younger ones in the mosque then when I'm not here?" Dilawar stated.

"I am, but I'm told I look younger than I am. I'm certainly not school age," laughed Mustafa.

"Lucky me," replied Dilawar.

You could be very unlucky if what I'm thinking is right, thought Mustafa.

As Dilawar and Mashuum left the mosque, Maura Grainger took another photo of them as they walked towards the car in which she was sitting. It was so easy to catch images these days because people were always playing games on their phones. It didn't look like you were taking pictures at all and the quality of the pictures was excellent. You could then email the very same pictures to whoever you wanted to receive them — all using the same phone. Wasn't technology wonderful?

***

"You seem to have made a friend at the mosque today, Dilawar."

"You could be right. I've seen him before when I've been down here visiting, but today is the first time we've spoken at length."

"He's a good young man who regularly attends the mosque and he usually attends the lectures of Abdul-Azeem Tawfeek in the same room as the one I was using today."

"Really," Dilawar said "That's interesting."

"Is it?"

Dilawar paused for a moment, not wanting to give anything away.

"I suppose not. I thought maybe I could get an even deeper understanding of Islam if I was chatting to someone who had attended lectures by Abdul-Azeem Tawfeek. He's known for the depth of his understanding of the Qur'an, isn't he?"

"Yes, he is. Widely read and well-travelled, I believe."

The honking of a horn as an Audi Coupé passed them startled them both. They turned in tandem as a voice shouted at them, "Bloody ragheads!"

"See, Jadd. That's exactly what I mean. Why do they do that to us? What have we ever done to them?" anger now apparent in his voice.

55

"We must walk away, Dilawar. We have to be the better men."

Dilawar just shook his head and walked on in silence, too angry to even pretend to engage in conversation with his grandfather while his head was full of the conversation he'd just had with Mustafa. Dilawar wanted to be the better man, but he didn't think walking away or ignoring what was being said or done was the way that would be achieved.

Chapter Eight

"Thanks, Alan, your team's doing a brilliant job. Jo Jacobs tells me the quality of photos we're getting is great. We're beginning to compile a comprehensive picture of the people who are attending the Zakaria Masjd Mosque on a regular basis so anyone new does stand out. Sometimes, they're just visiting family, but there are others who don't seem to be. We're not sure what their purpose is," stated Adrian Smythe, staring at the screen in front of him where he was engaged in a face to face conversation with Alan Edwards, who was in charge of the Leeds office.

"That's good to hear, Adrian. The team are working long hours, always aware they may have outstayed their welcome in the area and been 'made' in the process. At the moment, there doesn't seem to be a problem but, as you know, that can change in an instant."

"Indeed, it can, as we all know by experience," replied Adrian, his face a mask.

"The other reason I wanted to speak with you is that I seem to remember that amazing technician of yours has some facial recognition software."

"Yes, it's very sophisticated and we have had great success with it. What's your interest?"

"Maura Grainger has taken some shots recently of an older man and a younger one who have been going into and leaving the mosque together, engaged in what looked like quite in-depth conversations. We've identified the older man as Mashuum Lodi, the Imam of the mosque, but we'd like to know who the younger man is and thought Jo could work the magic. We know young men are being radicalised in that mosque and it may just be that the Imam is involved."

"Well, if anyone can get a match, it's Jo. Have the photos been sent yet?" asked Adrian.

"They went yesterday, but Maura wasn't sure she'd clearly identified what we wanted, so I said I'd pick that up."

"No problem, Alan. I need to speak with Jo later today so I'll make sure we get the photos through the facial recognition program. Please let your team know we do appreciate the work they're putting in."

"Thanks, Adrian. I will do that. The other reason I wanted to talk with you was to ask if we have any information from the people that were picked up in Sweden and here in the UK following the intended bombing. Anything you've got could be of help to us."

"We're letting them sweat a bit at the moment. All they know is they've been held under the Terrorism Act 2000 so it's a waiting game at the moment."

"We can't afford to wait too long, Adrian, because we know they still have a huge amount of castor beans stored somewhere. In fact, they may already have made more bombs."

"I'm aware of that, Alan, but timing is of the essence here. We need them to feel isolated and unsure if we're to get anything at all from them. You know how these zealots think. We won't be leaving it much longer, though."

"Okay. Sorry. It's just that we seem to be floundering

again and we know the damage ricin in bombs can do. I hate to feel so helpless."

"No apology needed. We are on it and you'll get any information as soon as we have it. Okay?"

"Okay. Speak with you soon."

Adrian didn't reply, merely gave a brief nod and closed the program.

***

Ali walked out of the hall where she'd been taking the tai chi class with her friend, Geraldine. They were having quite an animated conversation about the new moves to which they'd been introduced in the session.

"What do you make of the new Qigong animal moves we've just been shown?" asked Geraldine. "I like the tiger one but struggle a bit with my balance on the crane."

"I like the tiger one, too, and I don't mind the crane, but it's the antelope one I find most difficult. I can't seem to turn enough and it pulls my back a bit. I suppose it's just a matter of time and practice before it becomes easier. I do enjoy the sessions, though, and I'm glad we're taught some new moves," replied Ali.

Ali had found it difficult to concentrate on the FfF website for any length of time that morning, so had been glad to take a break to go to her regular tai chi class. She always felt more alert and awake after the sessions and was even beginning to enjoy the standing like a tree move they did at the end of the session. She chuckled to herself.

"Okay, share the joke," Geraldine said.

"Just thinking about how much I'm enjoying standing like

a tree. Who knew?"

Geraldine laughed. "Come on, we've got time for a quick coffee before we take root!"

"Ouch," replied Ali, "don't think we're deep enough to have roots, do you?"

"This conversation's getting too silly; upwards and onwards to Costa. My cortado awaits."

***

Walking into her kitchen, Ali barely had time to sit down before her phone rang.

"Hi, Ali." It was Adrian.

"Hi, Adrian," Ali replied.

"Jo tells me you've had a look at the FfF website and you think there's a bit more going on."

"Yes, I do, but couldn't say what it was. I felt I wasn't getting anywhere with it this morning so was glad to pop out to my tai chi class to unwind. There's nothing like stretching and twisting your body to open your mind, as well as exercise your body. I just got in, as a matter of fact."

Adrian didn't say anything for a moment, but was momentarily disturbed by the thought of Ali's body stretching and twisting. Get a grip of yourself, he thought.

"Yes, good," he said curtly. "Well, I hope you can get back on the website and let me or Jo know if you find anything?"

"Of course; your wish is my command." The answer was out of Ali's mouth before she could stop herself. Now she felt she'd been silly and was annoyed.

"Okay. Speak with you soon," Adrian replied.

"Super Techie was it?" asked Dan, startling her once again, as she hadn't realised he'd come into the room.

"No. It was Adrian."

"And what is his wish?"

"Sorry?"

"You said, 'Your wish is my command'."

"Oh. He wants me to go back on the FfF website to see if I can get more information."

"Right."

"Are you okay, Dan?" Ali asked.

"Why wouldn't I be?"

Ali had no answer to that question so she shrugged her shoulders and said nothing, feeling that something was going on, but not sure what it was.

After a few minutes of a very uncomfortable silence, Dan turned and left the kitchen.

"I'm going into town to get a few things. Won't be too long," stated Dan. "You'll be here when I get back?"

"Yes. Where else would I be?"

No answer.

What the hell is going on with Dan, thought Ali and could find no answer herself.

Ali began to think about Dan and Adrian. Had they worked with each other as she was beginning to believe, or was Adrian, knowing Dan was away, just something he'd worked out? Ali didn't like not knowing and she knew Dan with his 'need to know' statement wouldn't clarify the matter for her. Initially, she decided to take a few minutes to think about any connection there could have been between the two men since they'd met in 1978. Dan was often away when serving in the army since that time and many of the places he'd been were in areas where there was unrest or fighting. Since he'd left the army, he'd been in various places, either shooting, or fishing, the last being in Spain, quite close to the border between Spanish and Catalan speakers. That was when people first became aware that Catalan wanted to break from Spain. Was that the link between Dan and Adrian? Was Dan observing what was going on at ground level and reporting back to Adrian? She couldn't see Dan breaking into places, following bad guys or fighting with them, but Dan was brilliant at observation, having worked in intelligence at various times in his army career. Perhaps she was beginning to see where the link could be between them? Ali decided she'd have to confirm her suspicions by subterfuge. How ironic that that's what spies actually had to do.

Chapter Nine

It took the few days, since Mustafa Younan had met with Dilawar Lodi, to confirm what he'd thought when he'd spoken with Dilawar that first day in the mosque; Dilawar was to be the next bomber. They'd had quite animated conversations in the small social room in the mosque every day since the first meeting and, as Abdul-Azeem Tawfeek hadn't returned, Mustafa felt it was his job to make sure Dilawar was equipped to do the job for the Prophet for which he'd been chosen. How to do that was what was troubling him. It was obvious to Mustafa that Dilawar wasn't aware that the bombs contained a deadly chemical agent that would kill him and everyone else in the area when they were detonated, so Mustafa would have to tread lightly.

The day before, Nasir al Din Beshara had been visiting the mosque. Mustafa knew that Beshara and Tawfeek were close friends so he was surprised when Beshara asked him if he'd seen Tawfeek? When he said that he hadn't, Beshara looked concerned. As Mustafa wasn't sure how strong the friendship was, he was loath to ask any questions. Beshara was an important man in the Muslim community, who travelled extensively and visited many mosques, so Mustafa didn't want to get on the wrong side of him.

"Come with me into the social room," Beshara stated, giving Mustafa no choice other than to follow him.

Once inside the room, Beshara gestured towards the same chairs Mustafa had used days earlier when he and Dilawar had used the room for the first time. Mustafa felt very uncomfortable.

"What do you know?" asked Beshara.

Mustafa's face paled as he tried to digest the question.

"What do you know?" Beshara reiterated, this time anger creeping into his voice.

Still, Mustafa couldn't speak. Beshara stepped forward without warning and slapped Mustafa hard across the face; a face now a picture of pain and astonishment, not dissimilar to the image in Edvard Munch's painting of The Scream.

Try as he might, Mustafa couldn't get out the words that Beshara wanted to hear.

"Bombs," Beshara whispered. "What do you know about the bombs?"

Mustafa flinched as Beshara again took a step towards him.

"I... I have made the bombs."

The expression on Beshara's face changed. "You need to tell me all you know and I will then tell you how to proceed." At this command, Mustafa leant back into the armchair and begin to speak, his voice barely audible.

***

It was fortunate that Mashuum Lodi, Dilawar's grandfather, had to go to Birmingham on the day before Dilawar was to return home. Mustafa had invited Dilawar to his house and he'd agreed. He hadn't wanted to go to Birmingham with his grandfather as that would have meant spending, at the very least, a long morning in a different mosque while his grandfather went about his business. Mustafa's invitation was warmly received.

"As-salāmu alaykum," said Mustafa, as he opened his front door.

"Wa alaykumu s-salām," replied Dilawar.

"Come in. My sitting room is in the front," stated Mustafa.

Dilawar walked in and sat in an armchair in front of the large bay window.

"Want a drink or anything?"

"No thanks."

Mustafa sat down and began chatting to Dilawar about going home and back to school.

"I'm looking forward to going back to school this time because we're going on a school trip. First, we're stopping at Dunkirk for a couple of days where we'll visit the battlefields from World War II and then on to Cologne. I think there are various activities planned for us, as well as the usual visits to the cathedral and places like that."

Mustafa thought for a moment. "Don't they call it the Kölner Dom, the Mount Everest of cathedrals?"

Dilawar laughed. "How do you know that?"

"I remember reading something about it; typical of Christians to big it up. It's just a cathedral, isn't it?"

"Yes, it is."

Neither spoke for a moment.

"You know, that Merkel woman, I hate her!" stated Mustafa, with some vehemence.

"Why?" asked Dilawar, not realising he was being drawn in, but a bit unsettled at how angry Mustafa sounded.

"Well, she's the one invites us into Germany then, as soon as things go wrong in her country, she lets the Christian rabble blame us for it all. Do you remember reading in the paper about some women being assaulted in Cologne Train Station? Muslims were blamed for that."

"I think I remember seeing it on the telly."

"Now we're being blamed for everything and anything in their country and the Germans want all of us Muslims out. Lots of us are being targeted for beatings and worse. They don't know us yet they hate us. Why? The Germans need to be taught a lesson, don't you think?" There was real anger in Mustafa's voice now.

"Well, I… I… was…" stammered Dilawar, aware that Mustafa was voicing things he'd said earlier to his grandfather.

"You were what?" asked Mustafa.

"I… I… I don't know what to do?" continued Dilawar.

Mustafa thought he had Dilawar on the hook and didn't want to let him off, but he knew he had to be careful.

"What to do about what?"

Dilawar looked at Mustafa, in his innocence, not realising that Mustafa was using Dilawar's youth and lack of sophistication to entrap him.

"Is it to do with Abdul-Azeem Tawfeek?" Mustafa asked.

Startled by the question and eyes wide with fear, Dilawar began to shake. "How did you…" his voice tailed off before he could finish.

Mustafa put his arm around Dilawar's shoulders and whispered, "I know because I, too, have been chosen by the Prophet and given a purpose from Him. We are together in this."

Dilawar began to shake even more. He put his head in his

hands as tears ran rivers down his cheeks. Mustafa hugged him more tightly.

"Don't worry. Together we can do what has to be done. Empty your heart of tears and then we'll begin."

Dilawar continued to cry for a few minutes then, spent, he moved away from Mustafa's claustrophobic embrace.

Mustafa left Dilawar alone to compose himself while he went into the kitchen to make some tea. Returning to the sitting room with the tea, he found Dilawar ashen faced and silent, sitting well back in the armchair. Looking up, Dilawar took a mug of tea, said a cursory thanks and sank back into the armchair.

"What was the exact purpose you were given by Abdul-Azeem Tawfeek?"

Dilawar didn't reply so, after a few minutes, Mustafa tried a different approach.

"I was chosen by the Prophet to make something wonderful, using the talents He has given me," began Mustafa. "I know you're frightened at this moment, but I meant what I said when I said we were in this together."

Dilawar looked up, but still said nothing.

I don't know why Abdul-Azeem Tawfeek isn't back, but I do know what his plan was, so I am well able to help you in your purpose: the purpose of the Prophet." Mustafa stopped to give his words emphasis.

Still Dilawar said nothing.

"What I'm going to share with you could get me into a lot of trouble if you tell anyone about it, but I'm telling you so you know that what I say about helping you is true. Do you understand that?"

Dilawar gave a reluctant nod, thinking there was nothing

Mustafa could say that would make him feel less frightened.

"I have made bombs for Abdul-Azeem Tawfeek to punish those who stand against us!"

At this, Dilawar's head shot up.

"Yes, I can see you are beginning to believe me."

"How? Where?" Dilawar couldn't yet put a sentence together.

"In this very house; my parents are away a lot and I have my own space in the cellar to work on them. My parents never go downstairs and I am very careful what I say to them."

"Can I see where you work?" asked Dilawar.

"Of course."

Mustafa knew that if Dilawar saw the bombs waiting to be planted, he would believe anything else Mustafa said. Go gently, Mustafa was thinking. Dilawar didn't know what to think.

The door to the cellar opened noiselessly. Mustafa switched on the lights and began the descent into the cellar, with Dilawar close behind. He walked into the cellar, across the concrete floor to a door into a room at the far side of the cellar. Unlocking it with a key he had in his pocket, Mustafa stepped in, followed by Dilawar. Mustafa walked straight up to a long, oak table and picked up one of the water bottles from the table. It was a camouflage pattern, like a lot of boys had in their lunchboxes at school. Dilawar couldn't drag his gaze away from it.

"Were you to take two bottles with you on your school trip?" asked Mustafa.

Dilawar nodded his assent.

"Where were you to plant them?"

Dilawar was struggling to find his voice. "Cologne

Cathedral. When they go off, they will cause some damage to show that as the Christians don't respect Muslims, they can't expect Muslims to respect them and their beliefs."

"Do you know exactly where to place them?"

Dilawar nodded.

"One is to be placed at the Shrine of the Three Kings behind the main altar in the cathedral."

"Why there?" asked Mustafa.

"It's a richly gilded sarcophagus said by the Christians to hold the remains of the kings who followed the star to the stable in Bethlehem where Jesus was born. It would hurt the Christians the most there."

"What about the second one?"

"If I can get to it, the second one will be placed by the tracery balustrade of the Choir Chapel."

"What if you can't get to it?"

"Then, I'm to try for the train station next to the cathedral. It's called Köln Hauptbahnof."

"What if you can't get to that one?"

"It may be that I have to put two by the Shrine of the Three Kings. I won't know until I'm actually there which the best option is. One of them has to be the Shrine though."

"Do you have a specific time or day to place them?" questioned Mustafa.

"Late afternoon or early evening on the day we visit the cathedral."

Dilawar staggered slightly as if only now overcome by the magnitude of the task he'd been set. Mustafa put a hand on his shoulder.

"Let's kneel and pray that our purpose for the Prophet will be achieved."

Dilawar nodded and sank quickly to his knees on the cold, hard floor of the cellar.

Chapter Ten

Jim Adams was now sitting in the car in the street outside the Zakaria Masjd Mosque, snapping away at anyone who went in and came out of the mosque, while Maura was back at the safe house taking some time to sleep. 'Get it while you can' was their motto as things could change very quickly when on stakeout, and many times you'd get no proper sleep for a couple of days. Four to five hours at a stretch, sleeping when you're in a team, seemed like heaven to them. How sad was that, Jim, was thinking as he scrolled through the last lot of pictures he'd taken before he sent them off to his boss, Alan Edwards, with a copy of the same pictures to Super Techie in London. The very last one he'd taken had been of Nasir al Din Beshara as he left the mosque before getting into the back of a Mercedes which had been parked just a few steps away from the entrance to the mosque. To Jim, Beshara was just another face. If it had been Maura who'd been taking the pictures, perhaps she would have recognised Beshara immediately as the man who'd been driven to Leeds Airport by Said Ishak, before they knew Said was to be the bomber in Sweden? Who knows?

***

Shihab Ozer was feeling great. His leg was mended well

enough to go back on surveillance with his team, so today was the last of his light duties. His unfortunate accident, whilst trying to track Said Ishak in London, had been the cause of the painful leg and various bumps and bruises. In his determination not to lose Ishak, who they thought was going to get on a train to plant a bomb in Sweden, he didn't see the cyclist who'd just pulled out in front of him causing him to stand on the brake. Those were some very hairy moments, he was thinking, but all in a day's work. He was so glad to be going back to what he loved: the cat and mouse chase of villains.

"Anyone in there?"

Shihab sat up, startled.

"Thought you'd gone into a coma," laughed Josh Mitchell, the duty sergeant.

"Sorry, I was deep in thought," responded Shihab.

"Got a floater reported, I'm afraid, so need you to take charge of the scene.

"Okay. What location?"

"Leeds Dock, close to the Royal Armouries. I've a PC there to keep people away and the forensic team is enroute as we speak."

"Okay. I'm on it."

Fifteen minutes later, Shihab was at the scene. The PC had done a good job of keeping the area clear and the forensic team were already suited up and beginning the extraction of the body from the water. Divers had gone immediately into the water to keep the body from floating away or doing any more damage to itself if it knocked against the wall of the dock. People did sometimes jump into the dock hoping to commit suicide, or fell in when they'd had too much to drink or too many other substances and got too close to the edge. However, the team had a bit of a shock when they realised it wasn't an accident they were looking at as there were chains attached to the body which was floating in front of them. A platform was lowered into the water and the body slid onto it; the raised sides of the platform holding the body in place. The chains were gathered and put at the bottom of the platform as far away from the body as possible because they were covered in oil. Once the platform was on the dock, the forensic team moved in and started their work, taking the chains off the platform before they began their grim task.

Shihab watched all this with a sinking feeling. Someone dumping a body and tying it down with chains didn't want it to be found. That much was obvious. It was just something about the body that struck a chord with Shihab. He walked closer to where the forensic team was working.

"How long has the body been in the water?" Shihab asked.

"I can't say for sure until we do all tests, but a while."

"How would you quantify 'a while'?"

The Tec looked at Shihab with some disdain but, before he had a chance to say anything, Shihab moved closer.

"We had someone undercover and he's been missing for a few weeks. I'm afraid we were thinking the worse and now we have this," whispered Shihab, pointing to the body, his face hardly able to mask his concern.

The Tec's face changed.

"Are there any identifying marks that would be obvious on the body? I can't pull the body about too much, you understand, but if there was something superficial?"

Shihab thought for a moment and then stated, "The person I'm thinking of was a Muslim, and a devout one too, but he had supported Celtic Football Club from being a young boy. He had a tattoo of that same club on the inside of both arms. About here," Shihab stated, as he pointed to the same points on the inside of his arms.

The Tec picked up each arm in turn, turned them over to look at the inside. There, a mite faded, but there nevertheless, were two tattoos of Celtic Football Club.

Shihab nodded his head. "I know it's not totally confirmed and won't be until you've done your magic, but I'm pretty sure it is him. I'll pass on the information, but ensure they know it is pending verification. Okay?"

"Okay," replied the Tec. "I'm sorry."

Shihab merely nodded and stared at the empty eye sockets of a body he knew in his heart to be Muttaqi Saladin; a brave man who had wanted to do what was right for his religion and his people and who'd ended his life in a river, in chains, with his eyes being eaten by fish. Shihab shivered at the thought. He now had the unenviable task of letting Alan Edwards know what had been found and he would do that immediately. Muttaqi's death had to be for something didn't it?

"Yes?"

Hi, Boss, it's Shihab."

"I didn't think I'd hear from you today. I'll be seeing you tomorrow, won't I, or is that what you're phoning about?"

"Yes, you will."

Something in Shihab's voice made Alan uncomfortable.

"You okay, Shihab? Are you not up to coming back tomorrow?" concern now in Alan Edwards' voice as he tried to identify what in the tone of Shihab's voice had given him cause for that concern.

"Sorry, Boss, it's just…" Then nothing.

73

"You still there, Shihab?"

"Sorry, Boss." After a short pause, Shihab continued. "I was called out to a floater today in Leeds Dock. I got a bad feeling when I saw the body so I spoke with the Tec there."

"And?"

"It looks like it's Muttaqi. About the same height and colouring and the same Celtic FC tattoo on the inside of each arm. Been in the water a while. Won't have the full picture until the autopsy's been done, but I believe it is him."

"Suicide?"

"Not unless you can tie chains around your body underneath."

"What?"

"The body was weighted down; chains underneath to keep it down. Someone didn't want this body to be found."

"But it was. Why now? Why now?"

"Well, that's the odd thing. The chains were covered in oil. Smelt like diesel actually. Why would you oil chains you weren't going to use again? You wouldn't care if they went rusty, would you? It looked like they'd snapped in places, so I suppose that's why the body eventually floated up."

There was no reply.

"Boss?"

"Sorry, I'm just thinking. Wasn't there something in the news recently about a spill of diesel between Leeds and Castleford?"

"Yes, I think there was."

"Okay. Will get someone to see what they can find on that story. You stick close to the body and see if anything else comes to light before a full autopsy has been done. Anything you think might be significant, however small, get straight onto me."

"Will do; what about Muttaqi's family?"

"We can't do anything about that until we have full verification. At the moment, for the family, no news is still good news."

"I will get back to it."

Alan ran his fingers through his thinning hair. It was never easy to lose a member of your team but, murder — which is what this was looking like — made it so much worse. You could imagine your friend or colleague frightened, suffering or in pain and then, dead. Often, you never got to know who committed the murder and were never sure why. What a world we live in, Alan was thinking.

"Bugger!"

Alan gave himself a few minutes to compose himself then, realising he needed to pass the information up the chain of command, he picked up his phone, pressed the speed dial and waited.

"Alan, what can I do for you?" asked Adrian Smythe.

"I've got some news. Not fully verified yet, but it appears Muttaqi's body has been found floating in Leeds Dock."

"When you say not verified, what do you mean?"

"It just happened it was the last day of Shihab Ozer's light duties and he was the officer called to the scene. He knew Muttaqi very well and he got a feeling that the body was his. He asked the Tec at the scene to look for some identifying marks and he found them."

"What sort of marks?"

"A Celtic FC tattoo on the inside of each arm. Although a Muslim, Muttaqi had supported Celtic all his life. He had the tattoos on the inside of his arm so he wouldn't cause offense to other Muslims, with Celtic being a club associated with Catholics. Don't think we'd find many, if any, Muslims with those, do you?"

"No, I don't. We'd all hoped he was still alive somewhere, but we were all beginning to fear he wasn't."

"What was odd was that the chains holding Muttaqi down were covered in diesel. There was something in the news up here recently about diesel escaping from somewhere and polluting the river, so I've got someone looking into that story. We may be able to get a better fix on where the body was dumped initially if we can find the source of the spill. It may not have begun its journey in the Leeds Dock."

"Okay, Alan. I'm very sorry about Muttaqi. It does sound like it's him. Let's hope we can use the location of the spill to find where his body was dumped. That may lead us to his murderers."

"Let's hope."

Chapter Eleven

"Ali. How's things?" asked Adrian.

"Good. What about you?"

"Could be better, but that's another story. Are you still monitoring the FfF website?"

"I am, indeed. It's very interesting at the moment. I've just been discussing it with Super Techie."

"Discussing what?"

"There were two separate messages that we'd both identified as significant, but we didn't know why. I thought they might be a code within a code about the bombs."

"Did Super Techie agree?"

"He didn't think there was enough evidence to support that idea, but told me not to be discouraged and not to ignore my gut."

"He's right."

"I know. Now, I've just decoded another message. Before it said 'the package is not wrapped yet' but now I've got one which says 'the package is now wrapped'. I'm trying to track the person sending the messages, but meeting some resistance. I've got one or two aces up my sleeve so we'll see. Even if the messages aren't about the bombs, they're very odd."

"Well, they could be odd but not about bombs."

"I know, but there's just something that tells me it is. Very frustrating I can tell you. Anyway, Adrian, did you want something specific from me?"

"Sorry?" Adrian's could feel the heat in his face and was glad he was in his office.

"You phoned me about the FfF website. Was there something in particular you wanted from me?"

"Yes, sorry. I wanted to know if you'd found anything different to Super Techie?"

"Not so far, but we did identify the same two phrases which, at the very least, were odd. I'm trying to get IP addresses of the two people having the conversations, which include the phrases we'd both identified, using some of my own software. If I can do that, Super Techie can activate the camera on the computers they're using and we might be able to get more of an idea of who's involved."

"Sounds like you're both on the same wavelength which is good. Keep up the good work and let me know if you find anything that you think might be significant."

"Okay. No problem." Then, just before finishing the call, "Oh, Adrian, almost forgot, Dan says 'Hi'."

"Hi to him too," Arian replied automatically.

Hmm, thought Ali. Not a flicker when I mentioned Dan. Definitely a link there; I've just got to find it.

Adrian was sitting, staring at the phone, wondering exactly how much Ali knew and how much of a fishing expedition she was having. He realised he should have reacted differently when she mentioned Dan, but he was caught unawares. No harm done, he hoped, but he'd have to be more careful in the future.

***

Jo Jacobs was processing the photos which had been taken outside the Zakaria Masjd Mosque and forwarded to her by Alan Edwards. The program she'd written was very sophisticated and could identify familial matches, people who'd made minor changes to their faces or hair and people who'd been identified previously. She had a huge database of images, with dates the photos were taken, the time and the place. It had taken her a long time to refine the program and there were times when she'd wondered if it would be worth all the time and effort, she was putting into it. Today was the day when she would know it had been worth it!

"I've got a lead."

"A lead?" asked Adrian.

"The facial recognition program has thrown up a known," stated Jo. "Coming out of the Zakaria Masjd Mosque three days ago was Nasir al Din Beshara."

"Where do I know that name from?"

"Do you remember when we had surveillance on Said Ishak and he drove someone to the airport? Shihab Ozer's team followed them and Maura Grainger managed to get some photos of the man Said was with at the airport."

"I remember now. In Maura's report, she stated she felt that Said was on some sort of training exercise at the airport, but we never did get to know what all that was about."

"That's it in a nutshell. Beshara was the man who was being driven and who got on the plane. We haven't had any photos of him since then. Why is he at the mosque now? Tawfeek isn't there, is he? Do you think he could be meeting the Imam?"

"Who's the Imam and what do we know about him?"

"Not a lot, but time for some more digging I think."

"Get back to me as soon as you know anything about the Imam."

"Will do."

"Do we know where Beshara is now?"

"No. Do you want me to chase up the details of any vehicles he has? We have the registration number from the Mercedes he got into outside the Zakaria Masjd Mosque. We could then put an alert out for the vehicles; a look, report, but don't approach scenario?"

"Do it, I want an update every six hours."

"I will get on it as soon as I get off the phone."

"Okay. Has Ali managed to get the IP addresses for the two people having the conversations about the package?"

"Not yet. The messages are short and infrequent. I suppose they hope the messages can get lost in the huge mass of evil on the website as their messages seem to be quite innocuous."

"You could be right. Ali's on it anyway and, as soon as she gets even one of the IP addresses, I should be able to activate the camera on that computer and see who we're dealing with."

"Okay. I won't hold you back any longer. Let's hope these are some of the clues for which we've been seeking."

"God willing."

That's a strange thought, isn't it, Adrian was thinking. Why do we bring God into it when we want help? Why would God be willing to help us, rather than anyone else? Strange.

***

Mashuum Lodi was wondering what was wrong with his

grandson, Dilawar. He'd hardly eaten anything and had been very quiet for the past couple of days.

"Are you okay, Dilawar?" he asked. "You're not sickening for anything, are you?"

Dilawar shook his head and gave a forced smile.

"Sorry, Jadd, I'm not looking forward to going back to school, that's all," Dilawar replied.

"It won't be long until you're up here visiting again and, don't forget, you've got that great trip away to France and Germany when you get back. That should be very enjoyable, shouldn't it?"

"It'll be very different, I'm sure," muttered Dilawar under his breath.

"What did you say? You know I'm a bit deaf so you have to speak more loudly."

"I said I was sure it'd be different."

"There then, no worries. Your dad will be glad to see you back too."

"Sure."

"Is everything packed and ready to go? We have to leave in twenty minutes to make sure you get to the coach station in time?"

"Yes, Jadd, all ready," Dilawar replied swiftly.

"Collect all your stuff and let's go out to the car. I can wash the pots when I get back."

Dilawar went up to his bedroom, slung his large rucksack over his shoulders and, gingerly, picked up his small bag, inside of which were two water bottles — well, two ricin bombs encased in water bottles — carefully wrapped in bubble wrap. The bag was to be kept with Dilawar at all times. A knock wouldn't set them off he'd been told, but Dilawar wasn't going to test that theory. It would be a tense journey home, he thought, and it was only now he was realising what a tense journey it was going to be on his school trip in two days.

***

Ali was in her bedroom doing some Ishibashi. She was flowing through the moves, stretching, twisting and turning and, generally, having a good workout. Ali didn't usually do much tai chi at home, but she was struggling with her concentration and feeling very tense, so she felt the moves would help. She finished her workout with the 'standing like a tree' move. It sounded a strange thing to do but, despite it sounding a bit odd, it did the job. Ali felt focussed yet relaxed. Who knew standing like a tree would be so therapeutic? She giggled to herself as she sat down.

"Sounds like something's amused you."

Ali jumped, startled. How the hell did Dan keep doing that?

"I've been doing some tai chi and finished with the 'standing like a tree' move. It tickled me to think that standing like that for a minute would be so therapeutic and I was wondering how you could politely drop that into conversation without people thinking you were strange."

Dan laughed. "You are strange," he stated, as he dropped into the seat beside her.

"I never said I was normal, did I?" She laughed, as she stared into his handsome face. "You're adorable," she muttered, kissing him lightly on the lips.

Dan pulled her close and, stroking her hair, whispered, "I know."

They both burst out laughing, hugging each other and enjoying the intimate moment.

Chapter Twelve

Arriving at Victoria Coach Station, Dilawar was desperate to go to the toilet. He hadn't wanted to get off the coach at the services in case his bag got knocked or in case he had a similar experience to the one he'd had when he'd travelled up. Affronted by youths, who wanted to make fun of him, or worse, was not on the agenda. Letting the majority of people get off the coach before him, he almost ran to the public toilets. Within minutes, he was sitting in Victoria Station, having a diet coke and thinking through what would have to happen on his trip abroad. Dilawar was very nervous and knew he would have to get his emotions under control before he got home as his dad would be sure to pick up on any nervousness. It was one minute to his train, so he slung his large rucksack over his back and carried the smaller one with care as he strolled down the platform. Soon be home.

Qusay was pleased to see his son coming out of the train station. Dilawar smiled when he saw his dad waiting, but Qusay thought there was hesitancy there.

"Had a good time, son?"

"Yes. Jadd's well and I enjoyed our time together."

Qusay looked at his son's profile, noting a slight tension in his jaw.

"No problems while you were there, then?"

There was a slight hesitation before Dilawar's reply.

"None at all, Dad. I'm just a bit tired, that's all."

"Okay. Good to have you home. I've missed you." When he got no reply, he continued, "Got to get your stuff ready for your trip too, but we'll do that tomorrow. I'm sure I've got everything that was on your list."

"Thanks, Dad."

Father and son walked to the car, both lost in their own thoughts.

***

Adrian Smythe was sitting at his desk in the office of Specialised Security Systems in London. Its position was perfect for the work he did for the government and the firm was a good cover for his particular area of expertise: both physical and electronic security. At this precise moment, though he wasn't thinking about security systems, his face was a mask as he read the autopsy report on the body pulled out of the River Aire in Leeds. It had been confirmed that the body was, as thought, that of Muttaqi Saladin, the undercover operative who'd alerted them to the possibility of a cataclysmic event being organised. The muscles in Adrian's jaw tightened as he read about the torture Muttaqi had endured before finally being killed. Two fingers smashed, probably with a hammer or brick he thought; an eye removed pre-mortem and the body a mass of bruises. Adrian closed his eyes for a minute, desperately trying to remain calm. He never could understand the need for such vile and vicious behaviour, such wanton torture. He shivered when he thought how much Muttaqi must have suffered and how frightened he must have been.

"Barbarians!" he muttered under his breath.

Adrian walked around the office, working hard to steady his breathing. He was going to interview some of the people they'd picked up in connection with the proposed bombing in Sweden and he needed a clear head. His phone rang, but he didn't bother to pick it up as he knew it was the car for which he was waiting. Adrian adjusted his tie, put the autopsy report in his briefcase with his other paperwork and then walked briskly out of the office and down the stairs to the waiting car.

Abdul-Aalee Khatib was sitting in the spartan room, becoming more and more nervous. Why had no one spoken to him? Why was he being kept here? He was just at a point where he felt he'd explode, when the door to the room opened and two men entered. The taller, slimmer man walked to the corner of the room and turned to face Khatib. The other man, the one obviously in charge, sat down at the opposite side of the table to Khatib and looked him in the face. Not a word was said. Khatib was somewhat disconcerted by this, but did his best not to show it.

Khatib was becoming angry, but he knew he had to keep calm so he wouldn't slip up. When the silence threatened to overwhelm him, he struggled not to say something, anything, to change the oppressive atmosphere in the room.

"Name?" asked Adrian.

"What?"

"What is your name?"

"Why are you asking for my name? Why am I here?"

"I need you to state your name for the file. As you're being detained under the Terrorism Act 2000, you have no rights. The sooner you co-operate, the sooner we can move on?"

"I don't know anything about this act or why you think

I'm involved, but I will co-operate. My name is Abdul-Aalee Khatib."

"Can you tell me why you flew to Sweden, stayed less than a day and then returned?"

Khatib was taken aback by this. How did the man know about his travel arrangements? Had his cousin, Said Turay, betrayed him? He was the one who made all his travel arrangements? Surely not, he was family.

"It was… it was just a short visit to see a friend."

"What was so important that you had to visit in person for such a short time? Surely you could have texted, face timed, even phoned?"

Khatib was not used to being treated in such an abrupt manner and he could feel his anger pushing up his blood pressure. Before he could frame an answer to the question he'd been asked, the man sitting opposite asked another.

"How well did you know Muttaqi Saladin?"

"I… Who?"

The man sitting opposite Khatib continued to stare at him, his eyes never blinking, and never leaving Khatib's face. Khatib began to feel very uncomfortable and began to shift about on his chair.

"Perhaps a photo will remind you?" stated Adrian, as he put a photo of Muttaqi on the table. In it, Muttaqi was dressed in traditional clothes and he was smiling. Khatib looked at it, but said nothing. He was trying to work out how much the man sitting opposite knew and how much he could say without compromising his position.

"Perhaps a more recent photo would help?" Adrian said, as he put one of the autopsy photos of Muttaqi on the table.

Khatib looked down at the photo and his face immediately

drained of colour.

"I don't… I can't…" he shouted, jumping to his feet. He began to shake, eyes white with fear and, before he could say any more, he collapsed.

Adrian remained calm. He felt for a pulse in Khatib's neck and, finding one, he turned Khatib into the recovery position. The other man in the room had immediately phoned for the doctor on call in the centre and was, at that precise moment, updating him on what had happened. Within minutes, the doctor and two medics had arrived. The doctor checked Khatib's vitals, gave him an injection and directed the medics to take Khatib back to his cell, giving clear instructions on times Khatib was to be observed, blood pressure taken etc. The doctor would also be visiting, as required. Adrian left the room, went into the toilets and washed his hands, trying to calm his own growing anger at the duplicity of Khatib and men like him. He was wondering what result he would get when he interviewed Abdul-Azeem Tawfeek. Soon know, he thought, as he made his way to the other interview room.

When Adrian opened the door to the next room, he was surprised, although his face didn't show it, to see Abdul-Azeem Tawfeek asleep in the chair; or pretending to be asleep. Adrian kicked the chair as he passed, causing Tawfeek to sit up, startled.

"What? What's happening?" Tawfeek asked, trying hard to make his voice sound scared.

Adrian sat at the opposite side of the table, looked up and, without blinking, stared for about a minute into Tawfeek's face. The man with him went again into the corner of the room, facing Tawfeek.

"Name?" asked Adrian.

"What?"

"What is your name?"

"Why are you asking my name? Why am I here?"

"I need you to state your name for the file. As you're being detained under the Terrorism Act 2000, you have no rights. The sooner you co-operate, the sooner we can move on?"

"Terrorism Act? Me? Not me? I'm a devout Muslim. I don't know anything about terrorism," replied Tawfeek, in his meekest voice.

"Name?"

"But…"

Adrian cut him off before he could say anything else. "Name?"

Tawfeek seemed to realise his act wasn't working, so he tried another way.

"Sorry. I'm sorry. It's just that I don't understand what's happening. Of course, I'll give my name. It's Abdul-Azeem Tawfeek."

"Which mosque do you attend?"

"The Zakaria Masjd Mosque, usually. Why do you want to know?"

Adrian stared again into Tawfeek's face. He could see in Tawfeek's body language that he didn't like being questioned. Probably used to always having the upper hand, I'll bet, thought Adrian.

"Someone who attended your mosque has gone missing." Adrian didn't say anything for a minute, but Tawfeek didn't seem bothered by the wait.

"His name was…" Adrian opened the file on his desk and looked to be checking for the name. "Ahh, here it is. Muttaqi. Muttaqi Saladin. Did you know him?"

"Should I?" came the swift reply.

"It's believed he attended your mosque."

"Lots of people attend our mosque. I don't know all of them." Tawfeek seemed to be enjoying the exchange now, feeling he had the upper hand.

"I suppose you don't. Do you think a photo might help?"

"Perhaps."

Adrian opened the file again and sorted through the papers in it.

"Here it is," he stated, "thought I'd lost it."

The smirk on Tawfeek's face disappeared when he looked down at the photo of what was an obviously dead Muttaqi Saladin. He jumped up, pushing the table away from him.

"What is this? What are trying to do to me? I don't know who that is? Why would I?"

Although shaken by seeing the photo, Tawfeek was, Adrian was sure, in this right up to his neck. Adrian called for the guard to take Tawfeek back to his cell.

"You can't do this to me? I have done nothing?" he shouted. "You'll be sorry for this!" was all Adrian could hear of Tawfeek's angry voice as he was escorted down the corridor to his cell.

Adrian walked out of the interview room and went into the toilets where he scrubbed his hands, trying to erase the taint of evil he felt had emanated from both men. He wasn't successful. He decided he would leave Khatib and Tawfeek to stew for a few hours before he spoke with them again. Hopefully, by then, Khatib would be up to further questioning. Adrian felt that Khatib would be the weaker link rather than Tawfeek, who seemed quite in control. A couple of hours at the office updating his board may help them move a step closing to stopping the next incident and solving Muttaqi's murder. Adrian knew Jo Jacobs, aka Super Techie, was working flat out and that Ali was monitoring the FfF website so, between them, surely something would break.

Chapter Thirteen

Arriving home, Dilawar went straight to his room. He put the small rucksack on the top shelf of his wardrobe, making sure it was well-supported and wouldn't fall out when he opened the wardrobe door. He went to the contacts on his phone, found Mustafa Younan's number — filed as 'Y' in his contacts— and sent a Snapchat to him. All he typed was, 'Home safe'. He got an instant reply, which was just an emoji of a thumbs up sign. That's okay, he thought. At that same instant, his dad, Qusay, was looking at the two messages, courtesy of the mSpy software he'd put on his son's phone, and wondering what the brief messages were all about. He wondered if Dilawar had met a girl while he was at his grandad's, but discounted that idea quite quickly; he knew the only place Dilawar would have been was to the mosque. Must have made a new friend, was what he finally decided. Have to keep an eye on that, he thought as he walked into the kitchen to see what his wife, Anna, had cooked for their evening meal.

Upstairs, Dilawar began to unpack his large rucksack, putting anything that needed washing in the basket in his room. His next job was to get out all the clothes he would need for his trip, making sure he'd got everything from the list he'd been given at school. Strangely, putting the relevant clothes in piles on the floor proved to be therapeutic for him. Dilawar was pleased to see that he already had everything on the list, so no rushed shopping expedition would be necessary. He was glad of that because he knew his dad was wondering what was going on with him and Dilawar didn't want to give anything away.

"Dilawar, dinner's ready," Anna's voice floated up the stairs.

Was it that time already? Need to eat quickly and say little, Dilawar was thinking as he walked downstairs.

Twenty minutes later, and Dilawar was back in his bedroom; like an overwound spring ready to break. His monosyllabic replies at the meal had even made Anna raise her eyebrows. There was nothing for it, but to get down on his knees and pray. He'd been given a job to do for the Prophet and he wasn't going to let Him down. Dilawar didn't recognise the beauty of the prayers he was saying, so tense was he, but the rhythm of the prayers had a calming effect. Before he knew it, two hours had passed. It was too late to do much else, so he decided to spend some time on Fortnite, a game much enjoyed by him and all his friends. It crossed Dilawar's mind that when the bombs went off, if he was caught, people would presume that playing games like Fortnite were the cause. What a ridiculous idea that only old people would believe. He knew Fortnite was just a game, as most of his friends did, but it wouldn't stop people from blaming the software, would it? They couldn't possibly believe that it was because of something they, the old people, had done, spoiling the world in the process and not recognising the Prophet as the one truth, could they?

***

92

Ali Andrews sat back in her chair, running her fingers through her hair, something she did when she was tired. Her eyes were gritty after staring at the computer screen for so long. She hated the FfF website. Who the hell would want to be involved in some of the awful things on there, or some of the very stupid? Ali always tried to think the best of people and was sometimes proved wrong but, after looking on the FfF website, she struggled to clear her mind of the evil things she'd seen and read. There was no option though, she had to continue. It was only by sifting through the dross that she could find the coded messages, which she still believed were about bombs. Ali knew she'd have to take a break, however short, to eat and get back to a place where 'normal' life prevailed — whatever normal is.

A bowl of wonton soup and two cups of jasmine tea later, half an hour on Clash of Clans to clear her mind of the dross and Ali was back on the website. There had been some more messages while she was off the site. Her heart almost missed a beat when she decoded one of the messages — 'package well-wrapped and bird sailing soon'.

"Hi, Super Techie; have you seen the latest messages on the FfF website?"

"No, I haven't," came the swift reply. "I'm doing lots of searching for facial similarities and the like. Have you got something?"

"Yes. No. Maybe… Sorry, will start again." Ali gave Super Techie the message she'd found and the decoded version and asked her to check that the version she'd decoded was correct.

"Your decoding is spot on, but what makes you believe it's about bombs?"

"I think I recognise the keystrokes from messages we decoded when we stopped the bombing in Sweden. There's something familiar about them. I'm searching through the older messages and hope to come up with a match. I haven't found any matching IP addresses, but I really believe it's just a matter of time until I do."

"Okay. Not sure how much time we have, but I know you'll keep at it until you find something. Are you okay continuing on your own? I would try to help, but I'm swamped myself."

"Of course, I just wanted to keep you in the loop."

"You're doing great, Ali. I appreciate all your help."

"My pleasure," replied Ali, as she put down her phone.

"What's your pleasure?" asked Dan, who'd yet again entered the room without Ali hearing him.

"To keep searching for matches on that awful FfF website for Super Techie."

"That's okay, then," Dan stated, walking through into the kitchen and not pausing for a response.

***

Jenny Evans, of South East Today, was sitting in the staff canteen talking to her colleague and friend, Gwen Masters.

"We must have touched a nerve with our Mr Wooden last week," stated Jenny.

"How so?" replied Gwen.

"We've had a call from his PA, asking if we'd like to do a short follow-on from the interview."

"Really? That's a surprise. What's he offering?"

"He's asked if we'd like to be there when the children

going on the enrichment trip to Dunkirk and Cologne get on the coach. A sort of, look, we do take care of pastoral needs and provide some exciting opportunities."

"I'm sure he's always on the lookout to put a good spin on things. Isn't that what the CEOs are for in the academies?"

"I suppose so. Mind you, someone must have realised he's not the best for this type of coverage because he won't be there. The head of the school will be there to wave them off."

"I wonder if the head will be a more acceptable, caring face for the academy than Mr Wooden?"

"Well, she couldn't be much worse, could she?"

"Probably not," Gwen replied, unable to stifle a laugh.

***

Shihab Ozer was pleased to be back with his team, but he wasn't looking forward to his first job. Although he could have refused the job, Shihab was going to be the one to tell Muttaqi Saladdin's family that he was dead. Maura Grainger was going to be with him and both of them were dreading it. Muttaqi had a wife, a young son and an even younger daughter; his mother, eighty-six years old, was still alive and would have to be included. Shihab could have left it to someone else to give the bad news but he would have felt a coward if he'd have allowed that to happen. The problem was how much to tell them. Whatever he said, he knew he would cause them immense pain, but they had to be told. They knew he was missing, but they hadn't really known what his job was and how dangerous, so they would, perhaps, feel his loss even more acutely.

Ninety minutes later, Shihab sat in the office, totally drained. Shihab's wife had received the news in silence, her face contorted with the pain of grief, unable to speak, but rocking from side to side as if that could ease some of her pain. Shihab's mother let out a loud wail and then that awful keening sound that is made when people have had a great loss. The children were at school. Shihab and Maura had stayed and tried to give some comfort but were unable to say or do anything that stopped the rocking and keening. Eventually, Shihab's wife stood up, took Shihab's hands in hers and bowed her head. She then walked to the front door and opened it. As Shihab and Maura walked out the door, she whispered, "Thank you," then closed the door quietly behind them. Walking down the street to their car, they could still hear the outpouring of grief. Neither Shihab nor Maura said anything as they drove back to the office, each with their own thoughts.

Chapter Fourteen

Today was the day. Dilawar, awake before 6.00 am, took the time to kneel and pray. He thought back to his time at his grandad's, his meeting with Mustafa and his receipt of the bombs. He knew that he could wake his dad, tell him what had happened and his dad would make it right. Dilawar loved his dad, but he struggled with his dad's laissez-faire attitude to their religion. Islam was the one, true religion and Dilawar found it difficult to understand how his dad couldn't relate to that. Surely, he should want the world to be different because of it? Dilawar prayed to the Prophet that he would have the strength to complete his mission. Rising slowly from his knees, Dilawar went to get ready for his trip.

***

At the school, Gwen Masters was discussing the focus for the short film that Jenny Evans would have for South East Today that evening. She chatted to Mrs Williams, the head of the school, to get some background information which would be used as part of the questions. She seems a nice enough woman, thought Gwen, much 'softer' in her attitudes than Mr Wooden. Gwen gave herself a mental shake; she had to stop thinking of him as that. It wouldn't do if she slipped up and mentioned Mr Wooden instead of Mr Johnson, would it; however, she was sure Mrs Williams would recognise whom she meant?

The coach duly arrived and was parked up, ready for the young people to get on at the appointed time. Various stills were taken of the coach for possible use later. Copies would be given to the school to use in any promotional material they wished. By 7.30 am, the pupils who were going on the trip were filing out of the main building and lining up in reasonably straight lines. Baggage was put in the hold and pupils were allowed to keep one small bag with them on the coach. Once the main baggage was stowed, the pupils were arranged in a group and pictures taken. Mrs Williams was then interviewed with the group of pupils behind her as a backdrop.

"Good morning, Mrs Williams, and thank you for inviting us to the send-off of your young people," stated Gwen.

"It's our pleasure. As part of the Winning Ways Academy Trust, we work hard to provide both academic and enrichment activities for our pupils," replied Mrs Williams.

She got that in quick enough, thought Gwen. Need to offer more closed questions now.

"What's the itinerary for your pupils on this trip?"

"Well, as part of our safeguarding policy, I can't give you a detailed itinerary, but I can tell you that they'll be visiting Dunkirk and Cologne."

"Of course, you can never be too careful with safeguarding, but why those two places?

"In part, it's about the history of the two places and, with Cologne in particular, there's also the wonderful architecture. We try to give our pupils access to different cultures to help them understand and enjoy the diversity of life."

"Commendable, I'm sure," replied Gwen quickly, before Mrs Williams could continue. "What will happen when the young people return, as in, how will they disseminate what they've discovered?"

"When they return after the trip, they'll work in groups to do two presentations; one to the parents and one to the Year 9 classes who may have the opportunity to go on something similar next year."

"Sounds like a well-planned trip and one I'm sure the young people will enjoy. Thanks for inviting us."

"My pleasure. Our academy trust works hard to provide great opportunities for learning and enrichment, so we were happy to share that with you."

The camera continued to roll as the young people boarded the coach, scanning the passengers, not all of whom seemed to be enjoying the attention of the camera. Once all were on the coach and belted into their seats, the camera scanned the coach's departure, making sure to get in the smiling faces of the parents who were waving goodbye. Gwen thanked Mrs Williams again, off camera, while her team was packing up. The coach was soon on the M2 on its way to Dover where it was booked on the 11.10 am ferry which was timetabled to arrive at Calais at 12.40 pm. As they would be spending a long time on the coach while they were away, it was felt travelling on the ferry from Dover to Calais would be more enjoyable for the young people than their being encapsulated in the Channel Tunnel.

***

Mustafa Younan was glued to the television that evening, searching for a familiar face—and there it was. Watching South East Today, he scanned the faces of the young people who were going on the trip to Dunkirk and Cologne and was relieved to see Dilawar Lodi in the crowd. He was holding in his arms, the small rucksack Mustafa had given to him. Mustafa had no doubt that the bag contained the two bombs. What to do now? Abdul-Azeem Tawfeek still wasn't around. Mustafa wondered what he was playing at. Was he testing Mustafa to see if he could be trusted? Maybe, the test was to see if he could do something more important? You never knew with Tawfeek, so Mustafa was uncertain. At that moment, his phone pipped, making him jump. It was a Snapchat from Dilawar — 'On my journey'. Brilliant! That's what he'd told Dilawar to send if he was on his way and had the bombs with him. Mustafa knew what to do now; he had to let Nasir al Din Beshara know that the bombs were enroute.

***

Qusay Lodi, Dilawar's dad, looked at the screen message from Dilawar's Snapchat and was perplexed. Who was he sending that to and, more importantly, why? Was it to do with one of those games he was playing? As he was on night shift, he'd give it a couple of days to see what else was sent and, if he wasn't happy, he'd contact his dad to see if he could explain what was going on. Qusay knew it wouldn't be something bad because Dilawar was a kind and caring son, but there was something not quite right and he needed to sort it out. He was sure it wasn't anything urgent.

***

Dilawar was feeling sick. It wasn't the movement of the coach, it was not knowing what to do with the rucksack with the bombs in. He didn't dare put the bag on the floor in case someone kicked it. He didn't want to wedge it into the edge of his seat in case he crushed the bottles. That left him with the bag on his knee, which was going to be a nuisance as the journey went on. His friend, Zaigham, was sitting next to him and hadn't stopped talking since they'd left school. Dilawar kept nodding and hoped he was making the right noises in the right places. When Zaigham started talking, he was oblivious to everything.

"What do you think, Dilawar?" asked Zaigham, interrupting his thoughts.

"About what?" Dilawar asked.

"Have you been listening to anything I've been saying?"

Dilawar could hear that Zaigham was angry because of Dilawar's inattention.

"I didn't know I had to listen," stated Dilawar, keeping his tone light.

Zaigham turned to stare at him and then he laughed.

"Yeah, you're right. I do talk a lot, but this is something I really care about. Okay?"

A relieved Dilawar replied, "Of course. Now run through it again and I promise I will listen this time."

Zaigham smiled and began to speak.

***

"Specialised Security Systems."

"Hi, Adrian, I have some news for you."

"Jan?"

"The same."

Jan Michaels was a biochemist, somewhat of an expert on ricin. Adrian had spoken with her when they were made aware that someone was making ricin. She'd done her best to see if any of her colleagues were involved, but she'd come up with a blank. She had stated, however, that a talented amateur scientist could make it, but not at the potency a fully-fledged scientist could.

"We've done a lot of tests on the ricin in the bottles in Sweden; some of them quite hairy."

"I can imagine," replied Adrian.

"Well, the news is both good and bad. I'm about 99.9% sure that you're looking for a talented amateur, not a more experienced scientist."

"Where does that leave us?"

"Not sure. In your place, I'd be looking for a science facility where, perhaps, equipment has been stolen relatively recently. In an area, possibly, where people are buying NBC (Nuclear, Biological and Chemical) suits or equipment. An experienced scientist would have access to all that at work so wouldn't be buying it."

"Is that the bad news or the good news?"

That's the good news. If it was an experienced scientist, the ricin would be more potent and more stable. The bad news is that it isn't as stable because it wasn't made by someone with more experience."

"What exactly does that mean?"

"It means the ricin may break down more quickly."

"Does that mean if it's set off in a bomb it may dissipate more quickly before it can do maximum damage?"

"Yes, it could mean that. It could also mean that the ricin breaks down in the container it's in, before they try to detonate the bomb, so it could be released in a more confined space."

"Bloody hell!"

"Bloody hell's about right, I think. Sorry, Adrian."

"Not your fault, Jan, and thanks for all your help."

As he came off the phone, Adrian felt once again that icy finger of fear. How could people be so barbaric in the name of religion? He would never understand that, he accepted.

***

Adrian had Porton Down Laboratory on speed dial. "Hello, it's Adrian Smythe. How are we with the production of RTA 1–33/44 – 198?"

No pause for pleasantries from the scientist at the other end of the phone.

"Well, we're doing not too bad. We've been able to use the samples we were sent to refine the vaccine. We believe the vaccine we have now is improved. Being able to use it on people has helped us turn a corner. We're producing more and building a reasonable stock. Here at Porton Down we've been working flat out."

"You always do. I'm not sure if it helps at all, but I have it on very good authority that the ricin is not being made by an experienced scientist. It looks like an amateur scientist or talented science student."

"Damn that bloody internet!"

"Amen to that. Anyway, thank you and make sure your staff is aware of how much we appreciate all they're doing on this. Keep me in the loop if there are any developments."

"Will do. You need to do the same so we can keep on top of this, if that's possible."

"I will, as much as I can."

Chapter Fifteen

The journey to Dover was terrible for Dilawar. Not because of traffic, although there was a lot. Not because of the swaying of the coach, because that didn't bother him. There was a heavy knot of fear in his stomach, twisting and torturing him. His mouth was dry and his head was thumping. What would happen if the bomb went off early? What would happen if he was found with the bombs on him? Would he go to prison? A young and immature man in prison, that wouldn't be a good thing, would it? Well, not a good thing for him. He knew that. He'd seen it on the TV. Dilawar had to fight to keep his feelings under control and he was barely managing it. The heat of the coach, the loud noise from the others in the coach, laughing and joking, all contributed to his fear and unease. Getting off the coach when it arrived in Dover, waiting in line to get on the ferry all increased the tension he was experiencing. Dilawar couldn't believe that their coach had only been given a perfunctory check as it passed effortlessly through customs. I bet they thought we were just a coach of kids and what harm could we do, he thought? If they only knew. Then he felt angry because they should be checking everything and everybody leaving the country, to keep everyone safe. No wonder bad things happen!

Dilawar was so relieved when the coach was on the ferry and parked and they were allowed to get off. He hadn't realised that he'd been holding his breath and barely breathing. He was very nervous, mainly because he didn't know what to do with the small rucksack which held the bombs. After much inner turmoil, Dilawar decided it would be safer to leave the rucksack on the coach. He placed it on the rack above his seat, his jacket in front of it, cushioning it to stop it falling off the rack. He had a body warmer on over his shirt so he knew he would be warm enough on the upper deck of the ferry. Much relieved to leave the bombs behind, he followed Zaigham off the coach.

Arriving at the upper deck, they decided to have something to eat before going outside — A quick diet coke and cheese scone then outside to gaze at the waves lapping against the ferry. Although he couldn't have imagined before that he would ever be able to relax, soon he and Zaigham were laughing and joking and, for a little while, Dilawar forgot the predicament in which he'd placed himself. He was a caring young man and he didn't want to hurt anyone, so he would give some serious thought to where and what time he would place the bombs. The damage to the cathedral was to be a message to the world, he was told, to make people recognise the Prophet. No one would be hurt. That's what he'd been told. He believed it. Another innocent being used.

Dilawar and Zaigham had a quick walk around the decks of the ferry, looking at all the amazing things for sale. In the end, all they bought was some sweets and diet cokes for the journey and a couple of bottles of still water. They had only glanced at the itinerary for the trip, so weren't sure how long they would be on the coach before they stopped again. Sweets and drinks were always needed.

The public address system sounded, telling all passengers

of cars and coaches to go back to their vehicles. By this time, Dilawar was ready to get back on the coach, dropping into his seat with some relief. He would be glad when they were off the ferry and travelling towards Dunkirk. The ferry ramp dropped with a clang, startling Dilawar, whose nerves were already frayed. The vehicles were shepherded off the ferry by men in high viz jackets and hard hats, who seemed able to move the lines with surprising speed and precision, like an intimate dance. Dilawar was amazed at the spectacle and somewhat in awe of the men who could manage such an operation with ease.

Out of the ferry at Calais and onto the Rue du Four À Chaux and the D245 towards the A16, which would lead to Dunkirk. Very quickly, they were on the A16 and moving towards the Avenue du Stade in Couderkerque-Branche, then onto the Avenue du Stade and Boulevard Alexandree III in Dunkirk. There was some traffic, but it was flowing and within forty-five minutes they had arrived at their destination and were disembarking from the coach.

"It's going to be an exciting few days," stated the teacher, casting a glance around the crowd of boys, "so enjoy them! Get your bags off the coach and into the hostel; once we've got that sorted out, we can begin our adventure."

"Yes!" came the swift reply from all the boys. All except one.

Chapter Sixteen

"Right, as we're very close to the beach, we're going to walk around in small groups, observing what the beach and surrounding area of Malo-les-Bains is like today. You need to make notes on your iPads and take any pictures that you feel may be relevant. Remember, you'll have to do two presentations once we get back to school, so the more information and pictures you've got, the easier that will be. Everyone okay with that?" asked the lead teacher, Mr Andrews.

"Sir," replied Zaigham, "how is that relevant to the war?"

"Good question. We'll be doing the observations for a couple of hours, and then we'll break for our evening meal. After that, at dusk, we're going onto the beach to do some role play about what it was like during Operation Dynamo in 1940; to try to understand how the troops felt during that evacuation following the German breakthrough."

Mr Andrews paused to scan the group of boys in front of him.

"I hope I don't need to remind you about the sort of behaviour that's expected of you here. We're going to give you some freedom to go up and down along the beach. We, the teachers, will be positioned at various points along the 4km stretch of the beach, so we will be available if you need us. You should have our school mobile phone numbers in your phones, so you can call any one of us if you need help with anything. If you haven't, put the numbers in now. Groups should, ideally, be three or four but no more than five. Anything I've forgotten teachers?"

"Just that the boys have three hours to do this and should be back at this point by 6.00 pm," stated Mr Malik.

"A reminder, too, that if there are any signs or instructions in French, without an English translation, they can use the Google Translate app on their phone," added Mr Timms.

"Thanks, teachers. Any more questions?" asked Mr Andrews.

When there was no reply, Mr Andrews directed the teachers to their various positions and then sent the boys on their way.

"Good job," he whispered to himself, hoping that the trip would get off to a good start. He then moved off so that he was in his position, scanning up and down the beach. Each of the teachers texted him when they were in position, so all he could do was keep alert and wait, something he found very hard to do.

"Wow!" Zaigham exclaimed, pointing to a sign at the side of the beach. "Look at all the things you can do here: water sports, hiking, mountain biking, sailing, lots of walks and, the obvious one, swimming."

"Why are you surprised? It's one of the most popular seaside and tourist resorts. You did the research on the internet with me before we set off," stated Dilawar.

"I know, but I still didn't think it would be as good as this?"

"Why? Don't tell me you still expected to see beaches filled with bloody sand and pieces of dismembered bodies; gun cartridges stuck in the sand with damaged rifles? Dilawar returned.

"No… but… well… I just thought there'd be more evidence of the evacuation, I suppose. I feel a bit stupid now," Zaigham swiftly replied.

Dilawar didn't say anything for a moment and then he slapped his friend on the back. "No harm done. It's the sort of thing any idiot would have said."

"Thanks." Then as he processed what Dilawar had said.

"Hey, you wait 'til I get hold of you, I'll show you who's an idiot."

Dilawar ran off, laughing as he moved quickly along the soft sands of the beach, with Zaigham running behind him and, eventually, rugby tackling him. Both boys lay on the beach laughing, enjoying that moment of innocent fun.

"Sorry, I couldn't resist," gasped Dilawar.

Zaigham just smiled. He knew Dilawar meant no offence and he didn't take any; a joke's just a joke.

The boys got up and continued to walk along the beach. They soon caught up with the three other members of their groups who'd walked on and were standing in front of dozens of coloured beach cabins.

"Who'd want to live in such a small bungalow?" asked Wayne.

None of the boys said anything for a few minutes. Wayne was a great footballer who had many friends, but what he didn't have was a lot of common sense.

Jimmy, another member of their group, spoke first.

"They're not bungalows, Wayne; they're cabins, like the ones at Faversham, where you used to get changed into your swimming kit before you went into the sea."

"Okay," replied Wayne, "but the colours are great, aren't they? They remind me of something, but I can't think what it is."

"What's the story with Toby Morey, wouldn't you like to know…" sang Alfie, the final member of their group.

All the boys started singing it, laughing as they did.

"I remember now," replied Wayne, a huge smile on his cherubic face. "I loved that programme when I was little."

"You're still little," added Alfie, and they all laughed again.

Wayne took this in good part. He was only 1.68 metres tall and substantially smaller than the rest of the group. He was used to these jokes from his friends, knowing there was no malice in them.

After taking some pictures of the cabins, the boys took some of the beautiful villas that overlooked the beach, each wondering what sort of job you'd have to have to be able to afford one of those amazing homes. They sat on the beach and discussed that for a while, each coming up with a more amazing job than the one before; banker, footballer, Olympic skier, pop star and, finally, F1 racing driver.

It was Jimmy who stood up first, reminding the boys that it was almost time to be back at the meeting point. They decided they would race back, the last one back having to buy the others some sweets at the first opportunity.

"Ready, steady, go!" shouted Dilawar and off they went at quite a quick pace. Zaigham was the last one back and, although he wasn't happy about having to buy sweets, he knew that a deal was a deal, so he would.

Everyone arrived back more or less on time; you always get a group who's late, but this time it was only ten minutes so not bad.

Mr Bradley called the boys to attention.

"Okay. Now we're going to eat. We've booked us in and there'll be plenty of choice. There are a couple of things on the set menu but there are also plenty of vegetables, salad, cheese, cold meats and baguettes. There's also a choice of dessert. Drinks will be non-alcoholic and, again, there'll be a choice."

"But, Sir, French children get to drink wine with their meals," floated a voice from the back of the group of boys.

"You're not French," continued Mr Bradley. "Another thing to remember is the toilets. In most of the places we visit, they will be just a hole in the ground or a trough. You just have to be careful."

This information was followed by a groan from quite a few of the boys who were not looking forward to that aspect of the trip at all.

"Make sure, after the meal, that you do go to the toilet because we'll be coming back to the beach and we'll be out here for a couple of hours, after which it will be showers and bed. We've a busy day tomorrow visiting the Musée Portuaire followed by the Museum Dunkerque 1940. Upward and onward."

Like the Pied Piper, Mr Bradley walked off, followed by the boys; the other teachers sited at various points in the trail of boys with Mr Andrews at the end of the trail to make sure no one was left behind.

***

The noise in the restaurant was almost unbearable, but Mr Andrews could see that it was just regular conversations between the boys. He didn't want to tell them to be quiet as they seemed to be enjoying their food and engaging in discussions. What more could he ask from them? He knew that some of them might find the next stage on the beach rather harrowing, so he was minded to let them have free reign here so they would be relaxed.

***

It was not fully dark when they left the restaurant, but each of the teachers had torches to light the way. They wanted to make sure that all the boys could walk safely out of the light of the restaurant, into the dark and then onto the beach. Once they were on the beach, Mr Andrews began to give instructions.

"Find a place where you can sit comfortably, with enough space to lay down if you wish. Do that now."

Each of the boys did as they were told, settling onto the sand. The three other teachers sat at various points behind the boys so they could see all of them.

Mr Andrews continued.

"We've done this activity many times in drama before we've actually begun to play our parts. Can you remember what we call it?"

"Creative visualisation," said a voice from the middle of the group.

"Brilliant. Yes, creative visualisation it is. Can anyone remind me what we do first?"

After about forty seconds, hands went up. Mr Andrews pointed to a boy on the left of the group.

"Sir, we sit up straight and control our breathing. Then you give us instructions about what we're to visualise and you ask questions to help us get into role."

"Spot on! Well done! However, tonight, you have the choice to sit up straight and control your breathing or to lie on the sand and do that because I'm going to try to get you to visualise how the young men were feeling during the evacuation. I'm sure most of them would have been lying down and trying not to get killed but, if you prefer to sit up, that's okay. Right?"

"Yes, Sir."

"Close your eyes and get into a comfortable position." After a couple of minutes' pause, he continued. "Now, breathe in deeply, hold it and breathe out. Keep doing that until you feel relaxed and calm."

Mr Andrews looked around at the boys and he could see that they were all doing just that. In the quietest voice, he began to talk to the boys, asking them to imagine how the young men must have felt with bombs exploding, guns firing, men calling out in pain because they were hit, or in anguish and fear, wondering if they were ever going to get home. Some of them not much older than the boys themselves because they'd lied about their age to get into the war. Terrified young men. All these things were said in an even, quiet voice, reminding the boys to keep breathing deeply and focussing on what he was saying. After about five minutes, Mr Andrews flicked a button on his iPad and the noise was overwhelming. It was from the recent film of Dunkirk with the bombing, screaming, guns firing, with the horror of war. The body language of the boys changed accordingly, some of their breathing coming in rasps as they became fully immersed. When Mr Andrews stopped the noise, he could feel the tension in the boys.

"Breathe deeply, relax your shoulders… relax your arms… relax your upper body… relax your legs… relax your feet. Let the tension in your body go. Continue breathing deeply and, when you feel totally relaxed and in control, sit up slowly and open your eyes."

Ten minutes later, when all the boys were sitting up, the questioning began.

"How did you feel? What frightened you the most? What would you have done in their situation?" On and on the questions came and many of the answers came from the boys themselves. After about an hour, the session was finished and the boys were escorted back to the hostel; faces pale and drawn, almost as though they had experienced the actual evacuation. There was little talk along the way. Once in the hostel and showered, the boys were given either hot chocolate or a cold drink and they went to bed readily, exhausted by the events of the day. Many of them would have troubled dreams that night whilst others were untouched by the experience.

Chapter Seventeen

Adrian Smythe took some time to check on the status of Abdul-Aalee Khatib after his collapse during interview. Luckily, he hadn't died, thought Adrian. He wasn't really concerned about Khatib's health because, although he didn't yet have enough evidence, he was pretty sure Khatib was involved in the radicalisation of young men and the torture and death of Muttaqi Saladin, their operative. Adrian just knew how much paperwork a death during interrogation would generate and he didn't have the time for that. Or for the investigation that would follow to ensure Khatib hadn't been 'helped' to collapse. Khatib seemed to be responding to treatment so Adrian had decided not to speak to him again. Yet.

Abdul-Azeem Tawfeek was a very different proposition. From the information he did have, Adrian had worked out that Tawfeek was the main source of radicalisation at the Zakaria Masjd Mosque. Not enough evidence to prove that either, but Adrian felt they were close to finding the links. He only hoped they found them soon before another bomb, or bombs, were set off. The hairs on the back of his neck stood on end when he thought of what might happen if bombs containing ricin, made by a talented amateur rather than a fully-fledged scientist, were detonated. Catastrophe wasn't a strong enough word. The outcome of such an event was unpredictable but it would be bad, of that there was no doubt.

This time, Adrian was already seated at the table when Tawfeek was brought into the interview room. A momentary start was the only clue Tawfeek gave that he was disturbed by that. He looked to the corner of the room and showed no surprise that the same man as before was standing in the corner observing what was going on.

"Sit!" Adrian's harsh voice echoed around the bare room.

Tawfeek glared at Adrian and made somewhat of a performance of sitting in the chair opposite Adrian. If Tawfeek was waiting for the usual 'pleasantries', he was to be disappointed.

Almost thrusting the photo of Muttaqi Saladin which had been taken in the morgue into Tawfeek's face, Adrian, asked,

"Muttaqi Saladin. How well did you know him?"

"I'm not sure I did know him. As I said before, a lot of people attend our mosque and not all of them come regularly."

As if not hearing Tawfeek's answer, Adrian pushed another picture forward of Muttaqi Saladin, taken standing in front of the mosque. The photo was time and date stamped.

"Isn't that one of the days you are always at the mosque?" asked Adrian, staring into Tawfeek's dark eyes.

Stumbling over his answer, Tawfeek muttered, "I would need to check my diary. I'm not sure what day that is…"

Before he could say anything else, Adrian interrupted him.

"I can confirm it is a day you were at the mosque. We have a couple of photos of him there on other days in which you were in attendance."

Adrian sat back on his chair, never losing eye contact with Tawfeek. The silence grew until it seemed to fill the room.

Tawfeek was struggling to maintain eye contact with Adrian and realised he was losing ground. He did not like that feeling.

"If you say I was there, I was there. I'm sure you wouldn't lie to me, but I can't remember speaking with the main in the photo at any time." All this said with a smirk on his face.

"That's interesting," stated Adrian, "very interesting."

Again silence. Tawfeek tried to process what was being inferred.

"You have evidence of my talking to this man then?"

"Have we?" came Adrian's swift reply.

Again silence, thick and oppressive

After a few minutes, the door to the interview room opened and two guards stepped in. Adrian nodded to them and they took up position in the room. Without further conversation, Adrian and the man who had been observing left the interview room. Walking down the corridor, they could hear Tawfeek shouting about his rights but this time there was a trace of fear in his voice.

"Lovely," muttered Adrian, knowing that their tactics were paying off. "I'll leave him for fifty minutes and we'll go at it again."

"Okay, Boss."

***

In the hospital wing, Abdul-Aalee Khatib was propped up with pillows, various tubes snaking out of his arms and machines bleeping. He opened his eyes and was surprised to see Adrian standing at the side of the bed, staring at him.

"What... what do you want?" he asked, in a voice weak and trembly.

"The truth," was Adrian's reply.

***

Exactly fifty minutes later, Adrian re-entered the interview room and sat down in his chair. The man in the corner returned to his position and the two guards left. Tawfeek's face was red with anger, an anger he could barely contain. He was used to being the one in charge. The one other people were frightened to offend. Being on the other side of this relationship, if that's what it was, was anathema to him.

"How dare you do this to me?" You will pay," he spat, waving his fist in front of him.

Adrian ignored Tawfeek's outburst and continued as if he'd never left the room.

"You say you've never spoken with the man in the photo, Muttaqi Saladin, is that correct?"

Tawfeek was confused. He didn't understand why Adrian wasn't answering him or why he'd left him. What was he playing at?

"I'll repeat the question. You say you've never spoken with the man in the photo, Muttaqi Saladin, is that correct?"

At this point, Tawfeek didn't know what to say, so he didn't say anything, just glared at Adrian.

That pregnant pause, Adrian used it so well.

"We've got recorded conversations of you and Muttaqi Saladin on more than one occasion. What do you have to say about that?"

Tawfeek opened his mouth to speak, but before he could answer, Adrian continued.

"You're a liar. You radicalise young men and trick them

into doing bad things, like planting bombs or hurting non-Muslims. You don't care if they get hurt or worse and you don't care who else gets hurt in the process. You are evil and I am going to lock you away for a very long time. Your friend, Khatib, has been very forthcoming. Think on that."

The two guards were back and Tawfeek was half-carried out of the interview room, shouting and screaming.

Chapter Eighteen

Ali was pacing up and down, glaring at her computer, muttering under her breath, obviously very annoyed about something. She leaned into the screen on her laptop, still muttering, but now in some agitation and running her left hand through her hair.

"Argh! Why are computers never simple? Frustrating isn't a big enough word," she growled. "I hate, hate, hate that FfF website. It's so… so…" For once in her life, words failed her. "That's it! I need some fresh air — really fresh air — and some time to think." Muttering to herself, she moved swiftly up the stairs and got out her cycling kit.

"Dan? Dan? Where are you? I'm going for a ride. Do you want to come?"

Getting no response, she got into her cycling gear and flew down the stairs and into the garage. There was Dan, headphones on, singing tunelessly to some rather heavy metal music, while he cleaned the shotgun he'd been using that morning. Ali put herself in his line of vision but, even so, it took about a minute before he realised she was there.

"Hi. Going somewhere?"

"I'm going shopping. I think it'll be easier in Lycra."

"You're probably right," was Dan's reply. "Most things are better in Lycra, I think."

Dan managed to keep a straight face for about twenty

seconds, and then he had to laugh.

"Sorry, couldn't resist it."

"Hmmph," was Ali's reply.

"Not feeling the love?" asked Dan.

Ali stared at Dan and refused to be amused.

"Going for a ride," she mumbled, kissing the top of his head as she passed.

Dan continued to smile as she got on her bike and shot off down the road. He put his headphones back on, continued cleaning his gun and began the mournful lament he called singing.

Head down, legs pumping, Ali could feel the tension leaving her body. She filled her lungs with the cool, clean air and continued to increase the pace. By the time she'd got to the end of the track in the woods, she was feeling so much better. Getting off her bike, she unclipped her water bottle from the bike and took a long pull of water. Ali decided she would take a five-minute break before she set off back. The muscles in her legs felt a bit tight so she did some stretching exercises. Tai chi in the wild, she thought, as she adjusted her breathing, feeling calmer and more in control. Ali clipped the water bottle on her bike, got on it and set off again in a different direction. She was about ten minutes away from home when the bike became cumbersome. She pulled over and checked the tires.

"Bugger! A puncture!"

Ali got out her kit and began to mend her puncture. She was just getting up when she heard her name called.

"A puncture? That's a pain. What, no Dan here to do it?" asked James, the scaffolder, who was walking towards her.

"I don't need Dan to fix a puncture, James. I'm quite

capable of doing it myself," came her tart reply.

James laughed. "I know that, but it would be better him getting his hands dirty than you, eh?"

"You're not wrong. Sorry, James, I'm just a bit grumpy."

"No worries. Tell your man I'll see him on Wednesday."

Ali nodded. She watched James walk away. She could see that he was struggling and remembered that he had some problems with his knees. You wouldn't believe he was a Third Dan in karate. Is anyone what they seem, she thought?

The puncture mended, Ali was soon home. Dan was no longer in the garage, he was in the kitchen and he'd made some lunch for her, which made her feel a bit guilty.

"Sorry I was such a grouch when I left, but that damn website is driving me mad. Not your fault though."

"No worries. I feel your pain," he said, putting his hand over his heart, a mournful expression on his face.

That lasted for all of twenty seconds, before they both burst out laughing.

"You're such a dope," Ali stated.

"But I'm your dope."

"Indeed, you are," she replied, a smile lighting up her face.

Within an hour, Ali felt she was beginning to make progress. She deliberated whether to call Super Techie, or to plod on until she had something more tangible. As she was reaching for the phone, it rang, startling her.

"Hello, Ali, it's Super Techie."

"Wow, you must be psychic, I was just leaning down to pick up the phone to call you."

"That's a bit weird but, hey, what isn't these days? I'm calling because I'm really stacked up with work. I know you're on the FfF website, but I could do with some help on my face recognition program. Do you have any time to help me with that?" asked Super Techie.

"I could make some time. The website is driving me bats so having another thing to do as well would help me to feel that I was actually getting somewhere. Tell me what to do and I'll give it my best shot."

"Thanks, Ali. I really appreciate your help. My software is scanning all the info we've got to see if we can see any familiar faces. It's tedious but if we get a hit, it could point us in the right direction. It's in the cloud, so I can give you access to it all. I have a couple of car internal GPS systems to scrutinise and I need to be on that right now."

"Send me the link and I'm on it."

"Thanks. I've got that awful feeling again that we're so close to finding what we need but we may not find it in time. I just hope I'm wrong."

"Try not to let it get you down. We're all doing what we can. Maybe a different set of eyes will help while you do whatever you need to do."

"Let's hope so. I'll send the link straight away."

"Okay. I'll be right on to you if I find any matches."

"Great."

Ali heard the ping and settled down to see what she could do with the software. She wondered why Super Techie was looking so closely at the GPS system in two cars. How could that link to what they were trying to find? I suppose it's need to know, she decided.

Jo Jacobs, aka Super Techie, sighed as she put down the phone. She knew she was very lucky to have Ali helping her because Ali was a natural. She had had some training, but her main skills were honed gaming, scrolling and scanning throughout systems and software. The members of Jo's own team were highly qualified but, sometimes, they lacked that innovative, out of the box leap that someone like Ali made, seemingly, without much effort — horses for courses. Jo stretched, cracked her fingers, an unfortunate habit, and turned to the task in hand. Could she put Abdul-Aalee Khatib and/or Abdul-Azeem Tawfeek at, or close to, the site of the diesel spill around the dates in question? The dates of the spill of diesel between Leeds and Castleford had been confirmed and the actual source located. After the autopsy of Muttaqi Saladdin, the coroner had been able to give a good estimation of the time the body had been in the water. If Jo could put all that together, it would be a major leap forward. Adrian was depending on her so she did her best to clear her mind so she could immerse herself in the task at hand. As had been said before, time was not their friend.

Chapter Nineteen

Dilawar Lodi struggled to get out of bed. The session on the beach the night before had made him feel quite ill. He thought about the bombs in his possession and was glad that no one would be hurt when they went off. He had slept badly. Every time he drifted off, he could see the faces of the young men on the beach, screaming in pain and terror. He was glad to see the sun come up. Dilawar thought about getting up then, but realised it was too early so he settled back into his pillows and must have dropped into a deep slumber.

"Get up, lazy. Come on! We have to be down for breakfast in five minutes!" shouted Zaigham in his ear, pulling the duvet off him.

Dilawar gave a grimace and went to pull the duvet back over him.

"I'm not hungry. Go away!

"Mr Malik is going around all the rooms and anyone who's in them is getting a really hard time. Get up! You need breakfast as we're going to two places today, remember?"

Dilawar nodded his head, sat up, swung his legs out of the bed and walked to the bathroom, his clothes swept up from a chair by his bed as he passed.

"I'll be two minutes. Keep watch, and let me know if Mr Malik is coming?"

"Okay, but be quick. I'm starving."

Dilawar gave his face a cursory splash, did the same with his underarms, sprayed some deodorant and quickly got into his clothes. He flicked a comb through his hair as he was walking back into the room.

"Mr Malik's just gone into the room below us. Come on!" whispered Zaigham.

Dilawar pushed his pyjamas under his pillow, threw the duvet over the sheet and was out the door before Mr Malik could enter the room. Within minutes, he was sitting in a large dining hall having croissants and jam and a cup of very strong French coffee.

"Finish up, lads. Out the door and lined up ready to get on the coach in ten minutes."

"Sir."

Mr Timms was already outside when Dilawar and Zaigham left the hostel. He pointed to the end of the queue; they lined up with the others boys and were soon on the coach on their way to Museé Portaire. It wasn't very far away, but the teachers had decided that keeping all the boys together before they entered the museum was the better way to transport them.

The coach pulled up in front of a large building in the Quai de la Citadelle. As the signs were all in French, the boys were unsure where they were. However, one bright spark was already on Google Translate.

"This is the museum and it used to be a tobacco warehouse in the nineteenth century."

"Can we get fags here then?" came a voice from the back of the coach.

"Right, lads. A reminder of behaviour needed, is it?" asked Mr Andrews.

"No, Sir."

"Good. Off the coach as quickly as you can."

The boys, rather subdued, disembarked and waited for further instructions.

"Before we go into the museum, let's have a look at that tall ship over there."

The boys turned to see a very tall ship moored at the quay.

"It's got three masts and it's called the Duchesse Anne. It was built at Bremerhaven in Germany in 1901."

"Can we go on it?" asked Wayne.

"It's the only tall ship you can board for a tour in France but, I'm afraid, we haven't time to do that. We're here this morning and this afternoon we're going to the other museum. Sorry," replied Mr Andrews.

"I'm sorry, too, Sir. I think it would have been cool to have a go on it."

"I think you're right, Wayne, but we can't do everything in a few days."

The boys walked away from the quay, chatting about the ship and stood waiting to go into the museum. Before they went in, Mr Andrews explained that they would be escorted around the museum by a guide who spoke English, but that he would like the boys to at least try to use some of the French they knew. They didn't look very happy about that.

Two hours later, the boys were glad to leave the museum. There were thirty-five ships and a lighthouse inside the museum, but the whole museum felt rather bland to them. Cod fishing and whaling were not something which enthused them. Added to that, every sign was in French so Google Translate was being inundated, which detracted from any enjoyment they'd hoped to have. Once outside the museum, they had a slice of pizza and a drink from a small stand by the museum for their lunch. They were not feeling particularly inclined to visit the next museum, but dutifully tramped back onto the coach when told.

The Museum Dunquerque 1940 was a whole new ball game as it was devoted to the Battle of Dunkirk. The boys thought the artefacts were amazing. The rich collection of weapons was every boy's dream; you could hear voices become more strident as the boys became more excited at what they were seeing. Some boys were sketching the weapons, whilst others took pictures with their iPads and phones. There were lots of discussions about the uniforms and the models within the museum but, what surprised some of the teachers, many of the boys were completely in awe of the maps of the military operations. It was as if they had suddenly gained an understanding of real war. Not just a fight but operations that are planned to win battles and, eventually, wars. It was a struggle to get the boys out of the museum, so engaged were they with it.

Once on the coach, Mr Timms began to speak to the boys.

"I hope you've enjoyed the day at the museums. I don't think it would take too much intelligence to work out which one you enjoyed more."

"Too right, Sir."

"When we get back to the hostel, you're going to have a couple of hours on the beach, then our evening meal. You need to be in bed quite early because tomorrow we travel to Cologne. The journey will take almost four hours, so we'll be getting an early start."

A groan from most of the boys on the coach, but that was more about the early start than the journey. They knew, if they'd read the itinerary, that they were visiting Cologne Cathedral but they were also visiting Phantasialand, a theme park with some really thrilling rides, and Imhoff Schokoladenmuseum, a waterside museum devoted to, of all things, chocolate.

The coach set off and they were soon back at the hostel. Mr Andrews waited until off the boys were off the coach and then he spoke.

"You've got two hours to yourselves. There's a lot of beach and plenty of things you can do. I know we brought some footballs, bats etc., but if you're using them on the beach, make sure you're being sensible and not getting in the way of other people. There'll be three teachers on the beach at all times, but they're only there in case you need anything. You're old enough now to have some spare time. Enjoy it! Any questions?"

Total silence.

"Off you go then."

The teachers watched as the groups of boys set off in different directions, at different speeds and with differing intent. It is a brave thing to give youngsters extra freedom and could be fraught with disaster. But, how are young people to learn, if they're not given space? Mr Andrews was going inside for a coffee and, after half an hour, he would come out and replace one of the teachers. In this way, they'd all get a half hour break.

Most of the boys played team games, but Dilawar and his group decided to find a spot and chill out. Zaigham had bought the sweets he owed them for being the last one back the night before, so they sat eating them, talking about the day, specifically the weapons in the museum and discussing the next stage of their journey.

"You're quiet, Dilawar. You okay?" asked Zaigham.

"Yeah, just a bit tired, that's all," he replied.

"It'll be a bit more exciting in Cologne, won't it?" asked Wayne. "We're going to that theme park. I love those scary rides."

"Definitely more exciting," whispered Dilawar under his breath, a feeling of dread washing over him.

"You really are pale, man. It's nearly time to be back so let's make our way and sit by the return spot until it's time, shall we?"

"Sounds like a plan," stated Alfie.

Chapter Twenty

During the evening meal, Dilawar had managed to sneak upstairs and check the rucksack which contained the two bombs in the water bottles. Both seemed to be okay, so he replaced them and quickly returned to the meal. It never occurred to him that he wouldn't know if there was anything wrong with them. Ignorance is bliss. He sat down quickly at the table and was happy that no one had missed him while he was away. Dilawar, much to his surprise, ate well that night and had a bit of banter with his friends at the table before they all moved upstairs to go to bed. Although he didn't think he would, Dilawar slept deeply that night and awoke the next morning ready for the final stage of the journey.

Once he'd had his breakfast and packed his clothes, Dilawar walked down the stairs and out of the front door to wait for his friend, Zaigham. He'd done this deliberately so that he could do a Snapchat message to Mustafa Younin where no one would see him. The message read: Setting off for Cologne. End in sight.

***

In England, Mustafa received the message with glee. He was very pleased with the part he'd played before and was continuing to play. Mustafa was still uneasy about where

Tawfeek was, but he'd convinced himself that he was being tested to see how capable he was under pressure. He thought he was doing very well. Tawfeek had been away before for substantial amounts of time when no one knew where he was, so Mustafa was sure that was what was happening this time. Once he'd sent a quick update to Nasir al Din Beshara letting him know that everything was going according to plan, Mustafa settled back in his chair and began to watch some of that mind-numbing morning television you watch when you've no other options.

***

Qusay Lodi was just coming in from his night shift when he heard his phone ping. He looked at the message Dilawar had sent to someone, someone Qusay didn't know. He went cold. What's going on here? He really couldn't get his head around it. At the end of his shift, he usually felt pretty brain dead and craved the comfort of his warm bed and a good sleep. He was trying to process what was happening, but it was a struggle. Qusay knew he would have to do something, but for the life of him, he didn't know what. He decided to make a hot drink and then sit down and think through why he was so worried. Yes, that's what he would do.

An hour later, his wife came downstairs and into the kitchen and was shocked to see Qusay sitting there, pale and shaky, a cup of cold tea sitting on the table in front of him.

"What's going on Q?" asked Anna, Qusay's wife, recognising that he was in some distress.

Qusay looked up at her, his face a blank canvas. He mumbled some words, but Anna couldn't make out what he was saying and that seemed to panic Qusay. Like a chain reaction, Anna, too, began to panic.

"Are you in pain? Where does it hurt? What can I do?" Anna blurted out, not giving Qusay any time to answer as she rubbed his back.

"No," Qusay replied.

"No? What does that mean?" asked Anna.

For a couple of minutes, there was complete silence as Qusay stared at Anna, his distress now even more apparent.

Waving his hands madly in front of his face, Qusay erupted into a mass of incoherent mumblings. "Snapchat messages... Who is it? ... Don't know... Can't think... Dilawar... Who is it? Need to... Need to..."

"Stop!" shouted Anna, on the verge of a panic attack herself as she witnessed Qusay's demented behaviour. She leaned forward, enfolded Qusay in her arms, whispering soothing words into his ear and stroking his head. At first, Qusay's body was rigid then, slowly, he relaxed into Anna's embrace, small sobs wracking his body.

"It's okay. It's okay," Anna repeated, still holding Qusay in her arms. Once she felt he was more in control, she knelt down and looked into his face. He'd stopped sobbing, but the tracks of the tears were still visible. Anna had never seen Qusay cry and it frightened her. She stroked his face, stood up and perched herself on a chair in front of him.

"Start at the beginning, Q. Two are more powerful than one. Isn't that our mantra?"

Qusay looked into Anna's eyes and remembered all the reasons why he loved her. He could see that she was frightened, but he could also see that she was ready and waiting to hear what the problem was. He nodded, took a deep

133

breath and began to explain the order of events and why he was so troubled. Anna listened intently, the expression on her face becoming more serious as he progressed.

***

In Dunkirk, the boys were passing their larger bags to the driver to put into the boot of the coach. They walked round to the side of the coach and got on, choosing to sit in the same seats as previously. Dilawar was one of the last to get on. He had the small rucksack with him and he wanted to make sure he could put it on the shelf above his head, protected by his jacket. He didn't want it crushed at the back of the shelf.

"Okay, lads, we'll be under way in a few minutes. Make sure you've fastened your seatbelt before we set off. It takes about four hours to get to the centre of Cologne, traffic permitting, but we will stop about half way. Any questions before we set off?" stated Mr Andrews.

No one spoke.

"Okay, driver," said Mr Andrews, as he settled into his seat.

The coach progressed down Rue du Président, onto Boulevard Sainte-Barbe, then Avenue du Stade to the D365. After ten minutes, they were on the E40, making good time on the excellent roads. After about two hours, they stopped at one of the service areas so that the boys could do the usual toilet run, get something to eat and have a run around. Some of them had slept for most of the journey so were ready for some fresh air. After a short break, they got back onto the E40 for most of the journey. They took the turning onto the A4 to Opladener Strasse in Cologne. The final part of the journey was on the B51 close to Trankgasse, Cologne Central Station. Four hours and twenty minutes after they'd left Dunkirk, they arrived in Cologne at the hostel that had been booked for their stay.

Once they'd returned to the coach after being in the service area, Dilawar had begun to feel rather ill. His stomach was making strange noises and he felt sick. He tried to sleep, but every time he closed his eyes, he could see the wounded and dying soldiers on the beach in Dunkirk. He was feeling very stressed about what he was going to do in Cologne.

"Eaten something bad, Dilawar?" asked Zaigham. "Your stomach's making some disgusting noises. Not going to be sick, are you?"

"No, think it might be travel sickness. I'll be okay when we get there," replied Dilawar. "I'm sure I will."

Zaigham looked at his friend's pale face and he wasn't so sure. When they arrived in Cologne, he looked at Dilawar's face again and he really wasn't sure.

Chapter Twenty-One

Jo Jacobs, aka Super Techie, was scrutinising the report in front of her about the diesel spill in the River Aire. The chains which had been used to hold Muttaqi Saladdin's body in the river had been coated in oil — well, diesel actually — so if they could trace the source of the spill they could, she hoped, link that to the information in the GPS system of the cars belonging to Abdul-Aalee Khatib and Abdul-Azeem Tawfeek.

After an hour, Jo was developing a serious headache.

"Why the hell can't they write these in normal English?" she moaned to the empty room.

She realised she hadn't had a drink for quite a while, so she knew she was probably suffering from dehydration. She also knew dehydration wouldn't help her concentration. Walking to the water cooler, Jo couldn't help, but think of Muttaqi and how brave he'd been going undercover. She knew from Adrian's reaction to the autopsy report and his refusal to let her view it that the injuries must have been very bad. Muttaqi's funeral was next week and Jo knew Shihab Ozer would be attending. It felt worse for all of them because they couldn't tell the family why or how he died, even though, to them, he was a hero. That really didn't help his family, or his children who were now left without a father. Those thoughts were foremost in Jo's mind as she quickly drank two large cups of water and went back to her task, taking a cup of water with her to oxygenate her brain, she hoped.

The 8 mile stretch of the River Aire between Leeds and Castleford was the area where the spill occurred. As Jo continued to scan the report, she noted down anything which could help her search. The spill was thought to have come from Beeston and oil was first noticed at Water Lane in Leeds. The body was found close to the Royal Armouries Museum which was located in Leeds Dock. There'd been quite a lot of information in the report and Jo had sifted through it, identifying those as the most significant points. She took that information to her desk, brought her computer back to life and began to focus on the roads into and out of those areas.

"A comprehensive list, but manageable," she muttered.

Her next job was the time scale from the autopsy report. Although Adrian wouldn't let her see the full report, he did pass on the time scale given, so she could look at a specific period of time. She would make it a wider time frame so she didn't miss anything. As he'd had such a reaction during interview, Jo decided to scan Khatib's GPS system first.

"Time. Need more time," she whispered under her breath. "And I don't think we've got much."

***

Ali had just got out of the shower after her session of tai chi and was feeling much more relaxed. All the stretching and turning, concentrating on breathing and stillness and then the flow of the moves had contributed to a feeling of well-being. She quickly dried her hair and got into what she called her 'chilling' clothes. In these, she was comfortable and relaxed and could move around, sit on the floor, lie on the sofa or just sit and think. She knew she had to get her head back in the 'game' if she was going to be of help to Super Techie.

Much as she disliked the site, it was time to log back on to the FfF website on the Dark Web to see if any more messages had appeared. Although you weren't supposed to be able to trace anyone's IP address on the Dark Web, Ali knew it was just a matter of time before someone would write software to do just that. She, herself, had written additional software so that she was doubly protected. Her routine was to input her protection software before she logged on so she could confidently peruse that dark place without worrying about her identity being revealed. There were some very, very evil people on the Dark Web and Ali wanted no contact with them if she could help it. She'd put a bookmark on the last place she'd been, so was able to quickly get back into skimming and scanning mode.

"Whoever you are, you're a despicable human being," Ali muttered, with some vehemence.

"Who is?" asked Dan as he entered the room.

Ali sat back, startled, as she'd thought Dan was out.

"Have you been doing some sort of ninja training?" she asked, catching her breath.

"Ninja training?" Dan replied, and looked somewhat concerned. "It's a bit early to be drinking, Ali. Don't let this work you're doing for Adrian get on top of you and push you into drinking to keep fuelled."

Ali shook her head in frustration at the way the conversation was going. "No, I haven't been drinking. It's just... you keep popping up all the time and startling me."

"Oh. Sorry. I hadn't realised," stated Dan, after a few seconds. "So, which despicable human being are you shouting at?"

"It's that damn FfF website!" she replied, more sharply than she intended. "Some of the people on there are beyond belief. The things they put on that site are... well, I can't even think of a word that covers how bad they are. I feel sick sometimes just reading the things on there."

Dan dropped onto the sofa at the side of Ali and pulled her to him. He could see she was struggling not to cry — Ali didn't 'do' crying — but he could also feel the tension in her body.

"Breathe, Ali. Don't let it get to you. You're doing a great job; you always do. You will find what you need, just give yourself a bit of space." Then he just held her close to him until he could feel her begin to relax.

"I know. I know," Ali repeated. "You're right. I just can't get rid of this feeling of dread."

Dan kissed the top of her head, pushed her hair back and stroked her face gently.

"You will find what you need. I know you will. I'll go make you some jasmine tea while you crack on, okay?"

Ali smiled up at him. "It's a deal," she replied. "Any chocolate cake left?"

"I'm sure I can find you some," smiled Dan, as he walked into the kitchen.

***

In Teynham, Kent, Qusay Lodi had decided that the first thing he should do was talk with his father, Mashuum, to see if Dilawar had made any friends while he was staying with him. The phone was answered immediately, almost as if his father

139

had been waiting for the call.

"Qusay, my son, how are you?" asked Mashuum.

At first, Qusay didn't reply. Although he felt phoning his father was the right thing to do, he wasn't sure how to verbalise what he was thinking or what he needed to ask his father.

"Are you there, Qusay?" Mashuum asked with a note of concern in his voice.

"Dilawar — when…"

"Has something happened to Dilawar?" Mashuum asked, before Qusay could continue.

"I don't know…"

Anna, Qusay's wife, took the phone from him and pointed to the chair.

Qusay flopped heavily into it, his eyes empty and his face pale.

"Qusay, Qusay, what's happening. Tell me. Tell me," Mashuum's voice was trembling.

"Father, forgive Qusay. May I explain?" asked Anna.

"Of course, of course," came Mashuum's swift reply.

Anna recounted to Mashuum all that Qusay had told her. From the Snapchat messages on the phone, to Dilawar's tense behaviour on returning from his visit and now the final Snapchat message. Mashuum didn't really understand about the Snapchat aspect of the situation, but he got the gist of it and agreed that something wasn't right.

"Can you ask Qusay to leave what you've said with me, Anna, and give me time to think this situation through? It is too much for an old man to process straight away. I will ponder on it and ring back later today. I'm sure, together, we can work out what to do next."

"Let me talk to Qusay for a minute, Father,"

140

Anna turned to Qusay.

"Are you happy to give your father some time to think about Dilawar's visit and call us back later today? He needs to sit and think."

Qusay nodded his head in acquiescence.

"Yes, Father, we're happy to do that. We'll wait for your call."

"Thank you. You know how much I love Dilawar. I won't waste any time."

When Anna put down the phone, she turned to Qusay.

"There's nothing you can do at the moment, Q. If you sleep for a few hours now, you'll be better able to deal with whatever we have to do when your father phones back."

She led him gently up the stairs, helped him undress and put on his pyjamas and sat him on the end of the bed.

"In you go," she said, flicking the duvet over him as he lay down. Anna looked at Qusay's face and she struggled not to cry. Slipping under the duvet herself, she wrapped her arms around him and began to rock him gently. Within minutes, overcome by exhaustion, Qusay drifted into an uneasy sleep. Anna held him for a few minutes until her arms and back began to ache. She moved slowly away from Qusay and edged out of the bed, leaving him alone, as she hurried downstairs to await Mashuum's call.

***

In Cologne, the boys had unpacked their things, had a quick bite to eat and were lined up outside the hostel. They were very excited because they were going to visit the Imhoff Schokoladenmuseum and it was a relatively short walk from their hostel.

"Listen up, lads. The museum's only a short walk away and I'm sure you'll enjoy it," stated Mr Andrews.

"Will we get samples, Sir?" shouted a boy from the back of the line.

"I think you will but, please, don't be greedy. We don't want the last couple of days of our trip spoiled because someone decides to pig out on free chocolate. I'm sure no one wants to miss the day out tomorrow at the theme park, do they?"

"No, Sir!" chorused the boys.

"Let's go then."

Mr Andrews set off at a good pace and the boys, and teachers, had to concentrate to keep up with him. They were soon at the waterside museum, keen to get inside.

"Line up over there, chaps," shouted Mr Timms, pointing to the corner of the building, as Mr Andrews went into the museum to meet their guide.

The boys moved quickly, looking expectantly at the front entrance, pleased to see Mr Andrews coming back towards them within a few minutes.

"In we go. Remember, the staff speaks some English, but it would be polite if you tried at least a few words in German."

"Google Translate here I come," whispered a boy near the back of the line.

Most of the boys enjoyed the visit. They walked through a tropical forest, looked through the glass-walled miniature production facility, amazed at the speed of the processes. They were told the entire history of chocolate beginning with the Olmecs, Maya and Aztecs, right through to contemporary methods and production. Many of the boys found it fascinating, knowing how long chocolate has been produced and eaten and where. However, the things most of them enjoyed were the huge chocolate fountains and the chocolate truffles. It was obvious from the sounds the boys were making that they were enjoying the sumptuous quality of chocolate and free chocolate at that. For those who wished, boxes of truffles could be bought in the museum shop and a couple of boys bought some to take home for their mums. Whether the truffles actually got home is anyone's guess.

Zaigham was one of the boys who were fully entertained by the contents of the museum.

"Eat some, Dilawar, it's delicious," he stated, a huge chocolaty grin on his face.

"Thanks, but I think I'll pass as my stomach's a bit iffy. Think it's the change of water," replied Dilawar.

"Your loss," his friend replied, sampling yet another chocolate delight.

I'm not saying they had to drag Zaigham out of the museum, but it was a close thing.

Once out of the museum and back at the hostel, the boys had some free time. Some of the boys played games on their phones or iPads, some read and some had a short nap. Then it was out for their evening meal. Dilawar had little appetite. He didn't know if it was the change of water or if it was the fear of what he was about to do while he was in Cologne. Either way, he was glad to return to his room. Dilawar took a few minutes to check his water bottles before anyone else entered the bedroom. Everything is still okay as far as he knew. He would usually be very excited about going to a theme park but, this time, he just wanted that day to be over so he could plant his bombs and go home. It was an uneasy night's sleep for him.

Chapter Twenty-Two

Adrian Smythe stood in front of his whiteboard, thinking about all the information it held. There were various links already but there still seemed to be a lot of gaps. He could feel the frustration building because he knew, he just knew, that time was running out for them. He was contemplating his next step when the phone rang. Adrian picked it up quickly, hoping for some good news. He was to be disappointed.

"Yes, it's Adrian Smythe. You are?"

Adrian listened to the information, his expression telling the story.

"Thank you for letting me know."

Putting the phone down on the desk with some force, Adrian was overcome with a feeling of helplessness. He'd just been told that Said Ishak had starting having seizures and, during one of them, he'd banged his head against the wall whilst thrashing about. Within seconds, he was dead. Added to the damage previously caused by Nessa Wakim, an evil zealot, this blow to the head was one too many. The doctor had tried to revive him, but to no avail. Although Said had been going to plant bombs in Sweden, which would have killed a lot of people, he had been duped. An innocent used by evil men, supposedly in the name of religion. What religion believes it is okay to kill people? Bit of a stupid question, Adrian thought to himself, as he knew quite a few people who not only believed it was okay, but thought such killings were just! He wondered what could go wrong next. That thought had just popped into his head when the phone rang again. Gingerly, he picked it up.

"Just thought I'd let you know, Adrian, that we've got a fix on Nasir al Din Beshara. He seems to be doing a lot of travelling, which includes frequent visits to and from the Zaria Masjd Mosque. How do you want us to proceed?" stated Alan Edwards, the head of the Birmingham and Leeds office.

"That's a bit of good news, Alan," replied Adrian. "I want 24-hour surveillance on him and photos of anyone he meets. Anything significant, contact me immediately. Is it the usual team at the mosque taking the photos?"

"Yes, it is."

"You might have to add to the team now they have to incorporate surveillance on Beshara. Let me know if you need anyone else."

"Will do. Shihab's team is very experienced and they'll soon let me know if they're too stretched."

"Okay. Thanks for that, Alan."

Adrian put down the phone, feeling a bit more upbeat. He continued to stare at the whiteboard, hoping for a flash of inspiration or a lightbulb moment, to help fit all the pieces into the jigsaw that he saw in front of him. This was not his lucky day.

***

"Well, well, well," said Ali to herself. "What have we here?"

Ali looked at the message again and thought about what it could mean. She was sure it was about the bombs. She also recognised an IP address from her previous searching.

"Hi, Super Techie, think I've got something."

"Really, what is it?"

"A message from an IP address I remember from when we scanned before. It reads: 'Packages on final leg. End in sight.' Can you access the IP address and see who's actually on the computer?"

"Sure, text it to me now. I'll take ten minutes out from what I'm doing and see if we have any luck."

"Done."

"Keep chasing the facial recognition and I'll get back to you as soon as I can."

"Will do."

"What will you do?" asked Dan, appearing as if by magic.

"That's exactly what I'm talking about, Dan. You keep popping up. No wonder you're such a good spy."

"Me, a spy? Why do you think that?"

"Are you saying you're not?"

Before Dan could answer, the phone rang.

"Ali, I think you're right. I got the webcam working on the IP address you gave me and it's Nasir al Din Beshara receiving the message. He's had involvement with the Zakaria Masjd Mosque from the beginning. I can't trace the other end, the webcam's disabled; obviously, someone who's tech savvy at that IP address. Also, seems that IP address is redirected all over the place. It will take longer to sort that. I'm going to get on to Adrian now. Good call, Ali. Good call!" Super Techie almost shouted down the phone.

"Brilliant!" replied Ali, to an empty phone, as Super Techie had already terminated the call.

"What's brilliant?" asked Dan, his face showing some

understanding of what had just happened.

"I've tracked one of the people involved with the new bombs. Super Techie's getting on to Adrian now."

"Told you you'd find what you needed."

"I know you did. How perceptive!"

"More cake?" asked Dan, "or chocolate?"

"Think it'd better be Green and Blacks chocolate. I've got to throw myself into the face recognition software now and see if I come up with any matches there."

"Lucky escape," whispered Dan to himself, as he left to find the chocolate.

***

Mashuum Lodi had been to the mosque and prayed for help. He couldn't believe his grandson, Dilawar, was involved in anything bad but, from all Anna had told him, he knew something wasn't right. The words of the Prophet had always helped him to be calm and gave him time to work through any problems he'd had before, but even he felt that something was drastically wrong. What to do? What to do? He returned to his house and sat down heavily in his chair, not even bothering to put on the lights. Mashuum closed his eyes and tried to work out what to do. He must have fallen asleep because he woke up feeling cold and stiff, three hours after he'd returned home. When he awoke, he knew what he had to do; he would go to bed and get up early tomorrow to phone Dilawar. Mashuum knew Dilawar wouldn't lie to him.

***

"Hello, Anna. Is Qusay there?"

"Yes, Father, I'll get him to the phone."

"Hello, Dad."

"As salāmu alaykum," Mashuum greeted his son.

"I haven't time for that today, Dad. What do you know?"

"You haven't time to wish peace for your father?" spat Mashuum. "I don't know anything. I've made some discreet enquiries at the mosque and tried to find out if Dilawar became friendly with anyone while he was here, but no one seems to know of any friendships he may have made."

"So, what are we going to do? Contact the school, the police? What?" asked Qusay, his voice becoming more strident as he spoke.

Anna put her hand on Qusay's shoulder in an attempt to calm him, and it did seem to do so.

"I'm sorry. I'm just so worried."

"I understand," replied Mashuum, in a voice scarcely more than a whisper. After a couple of minutes, he continued, "I'm going to get up early in the morning and phone Dilawar. Whatever is happening, he won't lie to me. I don't think we should do anything else yet. We don't want him to get into trouble if we have misunderstood a situation. We know Dilawar is a good boy. He wouldn't be involved in anything bad, would he?"

"I'd like to think he wouldn't, but you don't know these days what pressures are put on the young. I think you're right though, let's see what Dilawar says to you tomorrow and decide what to do from there."

"I will phone you when I know anything. Goodnight, son."

"Goodnight. Sorry about earlier, Dad."

"Don't worry. It will be fine."

"Okay, wa alaykumu s-salām, Dad."

Mashuum finished the call and sat back in his chair. It was going to be a long night.

Chapter Twenty-Three

The next morning, Mashuum was up very early to pray before phoning Dilawar. He put down his prayer mat, knelt on it and began to recite some of the beautiful words of the prayers in the Qur'an. He was so involved in his prayers, that he lost track of the time. Loud knocking broke his concentration. It took him a minute or two for Mashuum to get his bearings and a couple of minutes for him to get up off the mat and make his way down the steep stairs. He could see the outlines of two people through the reinforced glass of his front door. The taller of the two was now knocking even more ferociously. Mashuum opened the door.

"Mashuum Lodi?"

"Yes, that's me. Why are you knocking so loudly on my door at such an early hour?"

There was no reply to his question. The taller man flashed some sort of identification at Mashuum.

"You need to come with us," he stated.

"Come with you? No. I have things I must do today, important things. Come back tomorrow and I'll go with you," replied Mashuum, closing the door as he finished speaking.

The taller man put his foot in the door to stop it closing and then stepped towards Mashuum who, instinctively, stepped back.

"You need to come with us, now."

***

Jo Jacobs had found nothing on the GPS in Abdul-Aalee Khatib's car so she'd moved on to Abdul-Azeem Tawfeek's; a car less well-travelled than Khatib's. After a couple of hours, she froze, not quite sure what she'd found.

"Gotcha! I believe I've gotcha!" she shouted to the empty room.

Without hesitation, she phoned Adrian.

"Need to Facetime now Boss," was all she said.

Within minutes, Adrian's face filled the screen. Jo noticed how drawn his face was and how lacklustre his usually piercing eyes were.

"What's the urgency? Some more good news, perhaps?" said Adrian, hopefully.

"I believe so. I looked at Khatib's GPS first because of his reaction when he was questioned and because he seemed to travel around a lot. I found nothing so was a bit discouraged. When I was looking at Tawfeek's, his journeys were mostly in the same areas. However, when I got to the dates we'd been given, the car had twice been in the area of the diesel spill, near Beeston. Although that put the car in the area, it didn't prove Tawfeek was driving it."

"Right, I get that. So what else did you do?" asked Adrian, sensing from the satisfied look on Jo's face that she'd found something substantial.

"I checked all the cameras on those routes for the dates in question and found two photos of the car. Guess who was driving?"

"Tawfeek?"

150

"Oh yes! I've sent the photos to your email address. They're date and time stamped too which is a great help, evidence wise, but I thought they might be just what you need to put that final pressure on." There's no doubt that it's Tawfeek driving, but there's someone else in the car, another man, and it's difficult to make out who that is."

"Well done, Jo. Good job. I'm back interviewing Tawfeek later today and I'm looking forward to seeing his reaction this time. What are you on now?"

"I'm going to get back on to the facial recognition software with Ali to see if two hands really do make light work."

"Sounds like a good plan. Keep me up-to-date with anything you find."

"Will do, Boss."

Adrian walked to his whiteboard and put the new information on it. Jo had rung him just as he'd finished putting on the information about the message on the FfF website to Nasir al Din Beshara, which was thought to be about the bombs. He stood back, trying to find more links between the increasing amounts of information it contained. Could do with Ali here, he thought. She's good with problem solving and I did enjoy working with her here before. He dismissed that thought quickly, did a mental check of what he needed to do and sat at his desk to contemplate ways forward. He knew he had another Facetime booked with the PM later that day and he wasn't looking forward to that at all, although he would now have some progress to share with her. Not sure it would be enough for her though.

**

"Dad should have called by now, Anna. I'm going to ring him," stated Qusay Lodi as he paced up and down, picking incessantly at a slight fraying at his cuff.

Anna could see that he was getting himself more and more worked up so she nodded her head in agreement.

"Perhaps you should, Q."

Qusay gave a sad smile, walked over to her and pulled her to him.

"I don't deserve you, but I do love you. You know that, don't you?"

Anna looked up at him. "Of course I do. Now go phone your dad. You'll feel better once you've spoken to him." She said all of this with a smile but, inside, she was worried. Mashuum was a calm and prayerful man, whose love for his family was epic. He said he'd ring and he hadn't. She didn't know what that meant, but she had a feeling that it wasn't anything good.

Minutes passed before Qusay came back into the room, his face a mass of emotion.

"What is it, Q? What's happened?"

"No reply on the phone. It just rang and rang so I called the mosque. They haven't seen him this morning, which is unusual, they said. Do you think he's had a fall or something? He could be laying in his house, bleeding to death. Or he could have had a heart attack or…"

Anna put her hand on his arm and he stopped and looked at her.

"Doesn't his next door neighbour, Zarrar, have a spare key in case he needs to get in for any reason?"

"Yes, and Dad's got one of his for the same reason."

152

"Perhaps you should call him and ask him to pop to your dad's to see how he is and, if he gets no response, use the key to go in and check everything's okay. It could just be that the phone's not working properly. At least this way we'd know."

Qusay tugged at his short beard. "It's a good job I've got you, Anna. I don't know what I'd have done. I'll go ring him now. His number's in our book."

Anna watched Qusay walk away to make the call and she felt sick. She knew it was worry and she knew she couldn't show it. She needed to stay strong for Qusay. Somehow, she knew he would need her even more with whatever was happening. Anna decided to make a hot drink for them. A cup of tea if not cures, at least helps, in all situations. Anna brought the tea back into the room and waited for Qusay. She could hear voices so that was a positive she thought. Wrongly, as it turned out.

Qusay was shaking when he came back into the room so Anna directed him towards a chair and put a cup of tea in his hands.

"Drink!" she commanded.

In his lethargic state, Qusay did as instructed. He then looked up at Anna and began to speak.

"Zarrar went around to Dad's and knocked on the door. He did it a few times and got no reply, so he went in. Dad wasn't there. Zarrar checked the whole house. Dad had obviously been there because the towel in the bathroom was damp and Dad's prayer mat was on the floor in his bedroom. Zarrar said he thought he'd seen Dad pass his window earlier, but he couldn't be sure. I thanked him and asked him to keep an eye out for Dad and, if he saw him, ask him to phone us. I didn't know what else to do."

Anna gave a deep sigh. She took a few minutes to think and then she said, "I think you should phone Dilawar to see if your Dad's phoned him. Perhaps Dilawar told him something that he needed to check before he called us."

Qusay's eyes seemed glazed as he processed what Anna had said. After what seemed like an eternity to Anna, he replied, "I think you're right."

Chapter Twenty-Four

Dilawar was not feeling well at all. He'd got up early and sneaked a look in his small rucksack. The bombs still looked okay, he thought, and he'd be glad to see the back of them. Just one more day. He went into the shower and spent longer than usual enjoying the spray of hot water. Once he'd cleaned his teeth, got dressed and styled his hair, he was feeling better. Ambling down to breakfast, he was surprised to find Zaigham already at their table, but not surprised to find him eating a rather large breakfast. The buffet style breakfast was one of the pleasures of life for Zaigham and he always visited it at least three times. Today they were going to Phantasialand, a theme park in Brühl, North Rhine Westphalia, so Zaigham wanted to make sure he was sufficiently fuelled before they had to get on the coach.

Looking at the mound of food on Zaigham's plate, made Dilawar feel rather nauseous. He decided that the best things for him would be bread and egg-based, with perhaps some cheese; water rather than coffee. Dilawar was sure that it was the stress of sneaking around with the bombs that was causing him to feel unwell and he hoped he'd be better once the issue of the bombs was finished and he could go home. How naïve.

"That's not much, Dilawar," stated Zaigham as he looked at the few pieces on Dilawar's plate.

"I'm not very hungry. Looked at what was on the buffet

and decided on some bread and cheese and some fruit. I don't want a lot in my stomach if we're going on rides. Projectile vomiting doesn't please anyone, does it?" came Dilawar's reply.

"Hmm. You could be right. I've only been twice to the buffet, but I think I'll stop at that."

"Good choice," said Wayne, unable to refrain from laughing.

Zaigham glanced at Wayne, gave him a scathing look and carried on eating. That was lost on Wayne who'd already forgotten why he'd been laughing.

Mr Malik had just finished his breakfast and was leaving the dining room.

"Enjoying the trip so far, boys?" he asked.

"Yes, Sir," the boys chirruped in reply.

"You need to be outside the hostel in fifteen minutes, ready to board the coach. Make sure you've all managed your ablutions by that time."

"Yes, Sir."

As Mr Malik left, Wayne was looking puzzled.

"What's up, Wayne?" asked Alfie.

"Umbrellas when it's raining," he replied.

"Ha ha — not," continued Alfie. "You look worried."

"Not worried. I just don't understand what Mr Malik said."

"He just meant make sure you've been to the toilet, washed your hands, you know?"

"Oh. Why didn't he just say that then?"

Alfie was just about to say that Mr Malik had said exactly that, but then decided it was no good continuing that sort of conversation with Wayne. It was the road to madness they'd all travelled many times.

The boys finished their breakfast and went to the toilet as instructed. They were out the door and waiting to board the coach within twelve minutes, with Mr Timms making sure they were behaving as they should. The doors of the coach opened and the boys were soon on board and ready to roll. Mr Andrews gave the usual talk about behaviour, Google Translate and health and safety, all before the coach set off. He advised the boys to make sure they had their seatbelts on at all times and then they were on the road.

Dilawar and Zaigham were looking up Phantasialand on their phones and comparing their findings. It seemed that there were quite a few thrill rides so they were trying to identify which ones they really wanted to go on. The Black Mamba seemed to be the one in which they were most interested, but some of the others looked very good too. They got fed up with searching and decided to look out the windows. Within minutes, they were both fast asleep, lulled by the rolling movement of the coach. They came awake quickly when the coach stopped and looked around to try and orientate themselves.

"Off the coach and line up, please," said Mr Andrews.

Once the boys were lined up, Mr Andrews spoke to them again.

"We're all going into the park together on a group ticket. Once inside, you'll be able to go off in your groups. We teachers will be in the park with you and we'll be available if you need us."

He paused, scanning the crowd of boys who, suddenly it seemed, were aware of the silence. They knew their attention was required. "How will we know if you need us?" he asked.

"We've got the number of your mobile phones in our phones now, Sir," stated a red-haired boy at the front of the line.

"Well remembered. We could keep all of you together, but that would mean you'd be queueing for ages to get on the rides. You're old enough now to be given some freedom and responsibility so, stay in your groups, enjoy yourselves and be back at this point in five hours. You've all got maps of the park so you should be able to move around and be back here by the time stated. You've all got unlimited bands for the rides, so the only things you'll have to pay for are any of the side stalls or any food and drink you buy. Anything I've missed teachers?" asked Mr Andrews.

"Toilets are clearly marked, but they're not as obvious as you think. Don't leave it until the last minute if you need to go to the toilet as there may be queues," stated Mr Bradley.

"Thank you for that, Mr Bradley; any questions, lads?"

"No, Sir."

"Off you go. Enjoy yourselves and be safe."

The boys nodded and were all soon on their way, moving swiftly through the park whilst trying to look cool and uninterested. Not an easy balance, but one some of them achieved.

***

Qusay Lodi was in a state of great agitation, pacing up and down in his front room and tugging at his beard. He couldn't find his phone. He'd had it earlier and he was sure he'd put it in the holder in the kitchen, but it wasn't there. Qusay knew, in some part of his brain, that his behaviour was over the top but he couldn't seem to stop himself. Heart pounding, head throbbing, he couldn't think what to do next, so he kept pacing, and tugging. Pacing. Tugging.

"Q, stop!" screamed Anna as she entered the room and saw Qusay's dishevelled appearance. He stopped dead, gazing at Anna as if he didn't know who she was, which frightened her even more than his appearance. She couldn't believe how quickly his appearance had deteriorated and how ill he now looked.

"What on earth has happened?" Anna asked, holding both Qusay's arms and looking into his face.

Again, the vacant expression, but no reply.

Anna shook his arms and put her face close to his.

"Q, Q, it's me. Talk to me."

Qusay continued to gaze at Anna then seemed to realise who she was.

"I can't find my phone," he almost whispered. "I need to find my phone!" the voice now more strident.

"Okay. When did you last have it?" Anna asked.

The tortured look on Qusay's face at this question made Anna realise she'd have to take charge of the situation.

"Don't worry. I'll find it," she stated, moving Qusay closer to one of the large armchairs.

"Sit here, close your eyes and I'll go and find your phone."

Qusay opened his mouth to reply but, unable to find a response, closed it again and sank back into the chair.

Anna checked all the usual places: docking station, top of the TV, window sill in the kitchen, hall table, but couldn't find it. She stopped searching and closed her eyes, thinking about all the places it could be and wondering how long it would take to search them all. She took a deep breath to stall the growing feeling of panic she could feel hovering on the periphery of her mind.

"Where could it be?" she murmured.

As Anna was thinking, she was moving her head from side to side, like a pendulum balancing the passage of time.

"Bedroom, I'll bet it's in the bed," she muttered, opening her eyes and striding purposefully up the stairs, two at a time.

That's exactly where it was. When she'd put Qusay to bed, he'd had the phone in his hand and it must have flopped into the bed as he fell asleep. Anna walked back down the stairs, wanting to enter the front room looking calm and in control, knowing that that would help Qusay to remain calm himself.

"Here it is, Q. You left it in the bed."

Qusay jumped out of the chair, startling Anna, who took a step back, aware of how fragile Qusay was at that moment.

"Thank you, thank you!" he shouted, hugging her and almost grabbing the phone out of her hand.

Qusay found Dilawar's number, pressed the phone symbol and waited to hear his voice. It rang and rang and then went to voicemail.

"Dilawar is not available to take your call at the moment. Please leave your name, number and short message and he will get back to you."

Chapter Twenty-Five

Abdul-Azeem Tawfeek sat rigid in the chair in the interview room, still the arrogant look on his face. He appeared calm but, inside, his stomach was churning. He hated all things Christian and all Christians. Their piety. Their caring Jesus. Their forgiving nature. Not for him those traits. Power. That's what people respect, power. Thinking about Sharia law brought a smile to Tawfeek's face. That law cast from hadith, the Prophet's words, and Sunnah, His actions; the Qur'an was just what countries needed. Tawfeek loved Sharia law because it meant no freedom of religion, of speech, of thought, of the press; no equality of peoples and no equal rights for women. Yes, Sharia law was about power and it was, in Tawfeek's opinion, just what was needed for England and all the other westernised countries with their debauchery and lack of respect. Islam was the one true religion and everyone who did not recognise that deserved to die. He was more than happy to be part of that process.

Adrian Smythe opened the door forcefully, causing Tawfeek to be pulled out of his reverie, startled by the noise. Staring into Tawfeek's face, Adrian could see the tension in his features. He continued staring until Tawfeek looked away.

"Muttaqi Saladdin?"

"What? Why are you asking about this man again?" replied Tawfeek.

Adrian didn't reply. He opened the file on the table and appeared to be perusing its contents. Tawfeek shuffled uncomfortably on the chair on which he was sitting, not knowing how to react to what was going on.

"Your car?" asked Adrian.

"What about it?"

"Who drives it?"

"I drive it."

"Your wife drives it?"

"No, she's not allowed," the answer out of his mouth before he could think.

"Why?"

By now, Tawfeek was very confused. Why was this man asking about his car? He decided not to engage in further conversation until he knew what the questioning was about. Tawfeek sat back in the chair, folding his arms across his chest.

Adrian returned to looking inside the file. He extracted some photos and put them face up on the table, in a line, in front of Tawfeek. He didn't speak for a couple of minutes.

"Your car?" he asked.

Tawfeek didn't answer. He looked at the car and wondered how he should reply.

Adrian continued with his questions.

"That's you driving." It was a statement, not a question.

No reply from Tawfeek.

"Who's in the car with you?"

"How do you expect me to remember? I use my car a lot."

"You're agreeing it's your car, then?"

Flustered, Tawfeek replied, "I didn't say that."

"Oh, I thought you did."

Adrian shuffled the photos and pushed them closer to Tawfeek, who shrunk back into the chair again, this time as if in retreat.

"Look at the dates on the pictures," stated Adrian. When Tawfeek averted his eyes, Adrian said again, "Look at the dates!"

Tawfeek jumped at the tone of Adrian's voice. He was searching in his mind for a prayer from the Qur'an that would help him, but he couldn't bring any to mind.

"On those dates, you and an accomplice, travelled to a specific point near the River Aire. On one occasion, you may have been scouting out the spot but, on the other, you were dumping the body of Muttaqi Saladdin. A body that had been tortured and abused then discarded like rubbish. The body of a courageous Muslim; not scum like you."

At this, Tawfeek jumped up, pushing the table back and scattering the photos.

"You have no proof of any of this. It's all lies. I want a lawyer. You cannot do this to me."

"Yes, I have and, yes, I can. Now tell me about the bombs," stated Adrian, ignoring the request for a lawyer.

Tawfeek looked shocked, but recovered quickly.

"I know nothing about bombs and I will speak no more."

At that, the door opened and Tawfeek was escorted back to his cell in total silence. Adrian would have liked to get hold of Tawfeek and really hurt him for his arrogance, for his actions to Muttaqi. For what Adrian knew was his murderous intent to harm all non-Muslims. Adrian stood up and left the interview room. He was going to interview Mashuum Lodi later in the day; a preacher from the Zakaria Masjd Mosque in Leeds who might also be involved in the bombings. Adrian needed some time before embarking on another interview, so tense was he after his time with Tawfeek. He needed a clear head and he needed to release the knot of anger that was gnawing away at him.

***

"What you got for me, Ali?" asked Super Techie, tapping on her keyboard with one hand while the other held the phone.

"Well, I'm still monitoring the FfF website and nothing further at the moment. My program's searching for places where large quantities of castor beans, mason jars and coffee filters have been bought have had no hits, so I'm thinking that the people making the bombs bought enough of everything at the time."

"Okay. Not sure if that's a good thing or not," replied Super Techie.

"I know what you mean. It's like waiting for a volcano to erupt, isn't it? You don't know when it will happen, but you know it will. I'm still running the face recognition software and hope to pick something up there. Soon, I'm hoping," stated Ali.

"I've been scanning the Leeds/Wakefield area to find any science facilities, including colleges and the like, who've had any equipment stolen in the past twelve months or so."

"Why?" asked Ali.

"We think it's not a scientist making the bombs, but a talented amateur. They could be a student, ex-student etc."

"Right. But why the search concerning stolen equipment?"

"Long story, short: a scientist would have his or her own

sealed cabinet at work and the relevant safety gear such as an NBC suit or a respirator. A talented amateur would probably not have access to those things so would have to steal or buy them."

"Oh, I see. Bit of a long shot though?"

"What else have we got?" asked Super Techie. "If we cover all the bases, we might get lucky."

"You're right. I'm not normally a defeatist. We just need to keep going, don't we?"

"Indeed, we do. Let me know if you get anything else."

"Will do. Back to the facial recognition stuff."

***

Dilawar and Zaigham were getting off the Black Mamba ride when Wayne came running up to them.

"Was it good? Is it worth a go?" Wayne asked, excitedly.

"It's amazing!" shouted Zaigham. "You need to have a go, doesn't he, Dilawar?"

Wayne looked at Dilawar, whose face was very pale.

"You okay, Dil? You look a bit out of it."

Dilawar was feeling quite wobbly after the ride.

"Yeah, I'm fine. Rides like this are not really my thing and my stomach's being a bit dodgy. Change of diet, I think. You should have a go."

"Don't want to go on my own, that's the problem."

"Zaigham will go on again with you. He loves it. I'll wait here and when you're done, we'll go on something else."

"Will you, Zaigham?" asked Wayne.

"Why not? The rockier the better. Come on then. You sure you're okay Dilawar?"

"Course I am. Go on or you'll miss your turn."

Zaigham nodded and ran with Wayne to get on the ride, shouting with excitement.

Dilawar sat down heavily on a bench seat nearby. He really wasn't feeling well at all. He'd be glad when he was back at home with this trip behind him. He zipped his jacket up and settled back in the seat to await the return of his two friends, totally unaware that in turning his phone off when they got to the park, he'd caused so much angst for his dad who'd been unable to contact him.

Chapter Twenty-Six

Sitting at his desk, Adrian Smythe was feeling under great pressure. His conversation with the PM earlier in the day had not gone well. She didn't seem to understand that they were doing everything in their power to find the prospective bombers. Neither did she acknowledge how difficult it was when you couldn't link all the evidence you had got. Adrian had tried to enlighten her on this matter but he'd failed. He'd seen from the set of her jaw that she was far from happy with the efforts of him and his team. The PM's final comments about bombs, devastation and loss of life oozed with her displeasure. She had made it abundantly clear that the responsibility for the safety of all concerned was his. A heavy load for anyone to carry.

In addition, the interview with Abdul-Azeem Tawfeek had not gone as well as Adrian had hoped. It was clear from Tawfeek's reactions that he was heavily involved in whatever was going on but he'd managed to contain his anger and not given up very much. Adrian had shocked Tawfeek when he'd asked about the bombs, but his recovery had been quick. Evil and devious is not a good mix. More evidence was needed and Adrian hoped he would be able to get that when he interviewed Mashuum Lodi later in the day. Adrian wondered, not for the first time, how people, who were supposedly religious, could be so evil. Surely religion should enhance your life? He was thinking about how involved this new person was in all that was going on in the Zakaria Masjd Mosque. Adrian knew Mahuum was a significant person in the mosque, but had been unable to find out much about him. Soon know, one way or the other, he was thinking, with a heavy heart.

***

In Teynham, Qusay Lodi was in an even more agitated state. Anna, his wife, was worried that he'd have a heart attack, so stressed out was he. Qusay had phoned his son's phone seven times up to this point and had left messages but, now, on the eighth time, the only response he got was to let him know that number now had a full mailbox.

"I will phone the school! That's what I'll do!" Qusay shouted, picking up the phone again. Before he could make the call, Anna took the phone out of his hand.

"There won't be anyone there to talk to, Q. Leave it until tomorrow and we'll phone first thing."

"What do you mean? They won't talk to me? Why won't they talk to me?" Qusay asked, anger now creeping into his tone.

"It's a school, Q. They'll all have gone home. The calls go straight to answerphone after 4.00 pm, to be picked up the next day, so you might as well wait until tomorrow and actually speak to a person."

Qusay didn't reply to this comment at first. He sat back in the chair, his head in his hands.

"It's my fault. It's my fault," he kept repeating.

"We don't even know if anything's wrong yet, Q, so how can it be your fault?" Anna asked.

"Dilawar didn't like that school much. He said most of the teachers were okay, but some of the other pupils weren't."

"What did he mean that they weren't okay?"

Qusay looked up at Anna before he spoke, his face a picture of grief.

"Dilawar is very respectful, as you know, and some of the other children aren't; even some of the girls. Dilawar said that some of them stay in a corner of the playground at some break times and 'mess around' with each other."

"Mess around? What do you mean?"

Qusay looked uncomfortable. "With each other... You know? Dilawar can't believe what little respect they have for each other."

"Surely not?" stated Anna, shocked.

"Not all of them, just a few. It upsets Dilawar because he's been brought up to respect himself and others."

"Did anyone tell the school about it?"

"No. How could I? I wouldn't have known how to tell them without being embarrassed myself."

"I understand what you're saying but, surely, there are child protection issues here?"

"Look, Anna!" shouted Qusay. "I've enough to worry about at the moment without worrying about all this. Surely their parents or the teachers or someone at the school should be making sure the children are all safe. Not me!"

Anna walked forward and put her arms around Qusay.

"I'm so sorry. It just shocked me to hear what you said. Let's sort out whatever's going on at the moment and, once we're all okay, we'll think of what to tell the school, okay?"

Qusay nodded his head and sat down again.

"You're right, I'll ring the school tomorrow and see if

they can contact the teacher who's on the trip with Dilawar and get him to phone me."

"Sounds like a good plan," said Anna, sitting on the sofa beside him, exhausted.

***

Ali was just taking a drink of her jasmine tea, when she got a ping on her laptop. Quickly putting the cup down so that she didn't spill it on her keyboard, she could see that the hit was from the FfF website.

"Bloody hell! Bloody hell!" she shouted. "Calm down. Get a grip of yourself," she muttered.

Ali checked the website again. She read the message, noted the IP address of the recipient and then sat back. She phoned Super Techie, but the number was engaged and she didn't want to leave a garbled message, so she decided to phone Adrian. He picked up at the first ring.

"Hi, Adrian, I've got something very interesting for you," stated Ali.

There was a momentary pause before Adrian replied. "Can't wait to hear what it is."

"I got a ping on the FfF website. The message was to Nasir al Din Beshara and it said that the package will be opened tomorrow."

"Have you spoken with Super Techie about this?"

"The line was engaged so I thought it best to let you know immediately. Super Techie identified Beshara, but she's been unable, as far as I know, to identify who sent the message. We're sure the package they're talking about is the bomb — or bombs."

"Bloody hell!" Adrian muttered.

"Couldn't agree more," replied Ali.

"Have we any idea of the location of the bombs?"

"No, 'fraid not."

Ali's laptop pinged again.

"Sorry, Adrian, I got another ping on my laptop. I will investigate and get back to you, or Super Techie, when I work out what I've got this time."

"Okay, Ali, thanks. I'll get on to Super Techie and let her know what's happening so she's kept in the loop. If the bombs are going to go off tomorrow it looks like we're too late to stop them."

"Let's hope not," replied Ali, but she was talking to an empty line.

***

In Phantasialand, the children were returning to the meeting point. Zaigham and the rest of the group were chatting and laughing about their exploits in the park while a very pale Dilawar stood feeling quite wobbly.

"Had a great time on that Black Mamba, didn't we, Zaigham?" asked Wayne.

"Yeah, it was so good. I liked it so much I had seven goes on it. Epic!" Zaigham laughed.

Wayne laughed. "I didn't do seven, five was enough for me. Any more and I'd have been meeting my hot dog again, or somebody else would."

"You're just gross!" stated Jimmy.

"I know," replied Wayne. "That's one of my good points."

The boys all laughed at the comical expression on his

face.

"What about you, Dilawar?" asked Alfie. "What did you like best?"

"It was all good," Dilawar shakily replied.

"You look a bit pale, Dilawar. You okay?"

"Just feel a bit off it, Alfie. I'll be fine once we're back to the hostel," Dilawar replied, with more confidence than he felt.

"I'll keep an eye on him on the coach and I'll make sure I have a sick bag to hand," stated Zaigham, looking at his friend with some concern.

Before any more could be said, the boys were herded onto the coach, quickly moved into their seats and settled back to relax on the journey back to the hostel. Although he hadn't intended to, within minutes of the coach setting off, Dilawar's eyes had closed and he'd dropped into an uneasy sleep. Zaigham glanced at him occasionally but, as Dilawar seemed to be fast asleep, Zaigham let him be, thinking that sleep was probably the best thing for him.

Chapter Twenty-Seven

Adrian Smythe walked into the interview room where Mashuum Lodi was sitting on a chair, eyes closed and body relaxed. He sat in the chair opposite Mashuum while the man who usually accompanied him walked to the corner of the room and turned to face Mashuum.

"Name?" Adrian asked.

"Mashuum Lodi," he swiftly replied.

Adrian waited to see what else Mashuum would say. After a couple of minutes, Adrian continued.

"You are being detained under the Terrorism Act 2000."

"Why?"

Adrian was somewhat taken aback by this question.

"We believe you may be involved in the radicalisation of young men who attend the Zakaria Masjd Mosque," stated Adrian, deciding not to mention anything about bombs at this point.

Mashuum smiled and replied, "No, you are wrong. There is no radicalisation there. We live and pray together, safe in the hands of the Prophet."

Adrian didn't reply to that statement. He sat and stared intently at Mashuum, who still seemed relaxed as he returned the stare.

"May I go now?" asked Mashuum.

"Don't you realise the seriousness of what I've just said

about you and your mosque?"

Mashuum seemed to be thinking. He rubbed his hand over his face, stared at the floor, closed his eyes and then he returned to staring at Adrian.

"You are wrong, my friend. We are about peace and prayer. I don't know what you're talking about."

It if had been Tawfeek sitting opposite him, Adrian would have been fuelled by rage at this point, but he couldn't help but feel that, true or not, what Mashuum was saying was what he really believed. Where to go from here?

"I need to leave now, but I'll return later and we'll continue this conversation. I ask that you think about what I've said and we'll talk when I get back."

"No. I must go. I have things to do. My grandson..."

Before Mashuum could finish his sentence, Adrian had left the room and he was being gently led back to his cell. Mashuum tried to talk to the man accompanying him, but to no avail. Once in his cell, he knelt and began to pray.

***

A string of messages was waiting for Adrian when he returned to his office. Nessa Wakim, the zealot who had been a key player in the proposed bombing in Sweden, had been found unfit to plead. She was to be placed indefinitely in a secure psychiatric facility. Adrian felt that was a good enough option for one as evil as her. Adrian was, however, saddened to see that her daughter, Meena, was to be put on trial and would, no doubt, be given a long jail sentence. Although she had been ready to assist in planting the bombs, she had been coerced into doing so by her mother, who had dominated and abused her, both physically and emotionally, for all of her life. Adrian wasn't sure what else the authorities could have done with her under the circumstances. She was another fatality really.

Jo, Super Techie, had left him a message confirming what Ali had told him about the message to Nasir al Din Beshara on the FfF website. Adrian wasted no time in getting in touch with Alan Edwards in Leeds.

"Hi, Alan, where's your team with Nasir al Din Beshara?"

"Hi, Adrian, he's still under twenty-four-hour surveillance — A well-travelled person. Why?"

"We've intercepted a message to him which seems to indicate he's a key player in the planting of the bombs. I need him picked up and brought to the cells."

"Under the Terrorism Act 2000?" asked Alan.

"Yep. Handle him with care. We're not sure if he has any bombs with him, if he moves the bombs or what, but he certainly knows about them. Of that we're sure."

"Okay. I'll pull the team off the observation of the mosque for a few hours so we can pick him up with full team."

"Great, Alan. Once he's here, we need the surveillance of the mosque to continue for at least a few more days. Have you enough operatives for that?"

"We have."

Adrian's next task was one he was dreading: telling the PM they thought a bomb was going to be detonated the next day. They didn't know where or at what time. He could barely wait!

***

Meanwhile, in Cologne, the boys had returned to the hostel.

Dilawar felt very wobbly so he decided he'd miss the evening meal and go for a lie down. He knew he could get something from the vending machines if he was hungry when he woke up. When the others went down to eat, he checked the rucksack which contained the bombs then put it away. He only intended to sleep for a couple of hours, but he went into such a deep sleep, he didn't even wake up when Zaigham came back into the room. Zaigham could see that he was fast asleep so he decided not to wake him, believing that a good night's sleep would do him good. He went down to the vending machine and got a bottle of water, some crisps and a bar of chocolate and put them on the table at the side of Dilawar's bed. He knew Dilawar would have done the same for him if he wasn't well. His duties as a friend completed, he went down to the games room, where he and some of the others were playing games until they had to go to bed. At 10.00 pm, they all returned to their rooms, jumped into their pyjamas and went immediately to sleep after their exhilarating day at the theme park. Tomorrow would be their last day in Cologne and they wanted to be awake enough to enjoy it. Dilawar slept on, oblivious to all else; his phone a silent tomb.

***

Anna Lodi was speaking to Zarrar, Mashuum Lodi's neighbour. He still had not seen Mashuum and he told her that there were no lights on in Mashuum's house. Anna thanked him and put down the phone, reiterating that should he see Mashuum, to please ask him to phone them. Qusay was asleep upstairs, overcome with fear and emotion, completely drained by the events of the day. There was still no call from Dilawar.

Anna was worried too, particularly with how Qusay seemed to be crumbling before her eyes. Something bad was happening and she couldn't envisage Dilawar being part of that. He was such a good boy. She knew he'd found it hard when she first starting going out with his dad and, when they decided to get married, she could tell he felt it was too soon. He missed his mother terribly and it showed. Anna, however, went out of her way to keep Dilawar's memories of his mother alive and he responded to her thoughtfulness. They got on really well and she loved him as if he were her son. Anna struggled to know what to do. Sitting on the sofa thinking, she lost track of the time. When she realised a couple of hours had passed, she couldn't believe it. Anna was cold, lifeless. Dragging herself up the stairs, she dreaded what was going to happen the next day and wondered if she and Qusay would be able to cope with it. We'll cope with it together, she thought: 'Always stronger together.'

***

Adrian sat at his desk, tie askew, feeling both frustrated and angry. Whilst on the one hand he could understand how worried the PM was about the bomb, or bombs, which could be detonated at any moment; on the other hand, he couldn't believe she didn't realise how much time and effort they were all putting in to try to find the bombers. Bloody politicians!

The buzz of his phone startled him. Adrian picked it up quickly, surprised to hear the voice of the chief scientist at Porton Down on the line.

"Bad news for you, I'm afraid, Adrian."

"You might as well hit me with it."

"Okay. As you know, making the RTA 1-33/44 198 vaccine is a process where a fragment of the ricin A-chain is modified to eliminate the toxic enzymatic property of RTA, increase it stability and maintain its ability to produce the protective immune response."

"With you so far."

"Your belief that the maker of the ricin was a talented amateur, rather than an experienced scientist, led us to look at the effect of the vaccine on the agents who were vaccinated. Using our results from that, we did tests on some of the ricin in the bombs using our current vaccine. We found from our tests that the ricin is unstable"

"That means what?"

"We're not really sure. It could break down inside its container and produce something not like the ricin we know, or it could become corrosive and eat away at the container in which it's held. We're not really sure."

"This just gets worse and worse."

"Well, it does and it doesn't."

"No riddles, please; I'm too hyped up as it is."

"Sorry, Adrian, I didn't mean to drag this out. The bottom line is we've produced a different vaccine that should be more effective against the unstable ricin; a similar vaccine, but subtly different."

"Are you saying you now have two vaccines?"

"Absolutely. We're making both and have a reasonable amount already made."

"That is better news. I was on the verge of phoning you because we believe the bomb, or bombs, will be detonated tomorrow. The problem is, we don't know where. What I was going to ask was that you have portable containers ready to transport the vaccines, to somewhere in Europe, we think, at what could be very short notice."

"We can do that, Adrian. You just give the word."

"Okay. I'll let you get back to your vaccine making while we continued to search for the bombers."

Moving to his coffee machine, Adrian was stopped in his tracks by the phone ringing again.

"Bugger!" he muttered as he made his way back to his desk.

Adrian listened intently to the animated voice at the end of the line.

"I'll be there in ten minutes. Have him waiting in the room please."

What now, he thought to himself as he put on his coat and made his way back to the interview room, stopping on his way to pick up the relevant paperwork. By this time, it was 10.00 pm and Adrian was running on empty.

When Adrian entered the room, the other agent was already standing in the corner looking at Mashuum Lodi, who was sitting erect in his chair. Adrian sat down in the chair at the other side of the table.

"You asked, or should I say demanded, to speak with me again. Correct?" Adrian asked with a harsh tone of his voice.

Mashuum nodded his head in acquiescence.

"I would like you to answer a few questions for me first. Okay?"

Again, he nodded his head.

Adrian put a photo in front of Mashuum on the table.

"Do you know this man?" Adrian asked.

Mashuum picked up the photo and studied it carefully.

"Yes. His name was Muttaqi and he visited our mosque a

179

few times, but I haven't seen him for a while."

"Did you ever speak with him?"

"Yes. He was a man struggling with something I think, but he seemed a good man. Has he done something wrong?"

"No, something wrong was done to him."

Mashuum looked confused. "I don't understand."

When the second photo of Muttaqi was put on the table, Mashuum's face crumpled. "Oh no! Who would do such a thing?"

For a few minutes, Adrian didn't speak, thinking about Mashuum's reaction to the second photo and the obvious distress Mashuum was showing as he looked at it. No one's as good an actor as that, thought Adrian.

"Someone in your mosque is responsible, but we don't know who."

"I can't believe that. I can't believe that," Mashuum repeated. "And you thought I could do this; be involved in this?" he continued, pointing at the photo.

Adrian took a minute before he spoke.

"I wasn't sure before, but now I am sure that you're not involved. I am sorry to have brought you here, but we are living in troubled times. You're a key member of your mosque and there are some bad things coming from there."

For a minute, neither of the men spoke.

"Why did you want to talk with me?" asked Adrian.

"Something is going on with my grandson and I don't know what to do?"

"How would I be able to help?"

Mashuum let out a huge sigh and he began to tell Adrian about Dilawar's Snapchat texts, his tense behaviour and his growing anger with the treatment of Muslims he was seeing around him. Mashuum told Adrian he was trying to find out from Dilawar what, if anything, was happening but he hadn't been able to call him because he'd been taken into custody. Adrian let Mashuum finish his story.

"Where is your grandson now?" Adrian asked.

"On a trip to France and Germany for a few days; I'm not sure of the exact itinerary, but he's visiting Dunkirk and Cologne."

Adrian had that walking over your grave feeling.

Chapter Twenty-Eight

Getting up from his prayer mat, Mustafa Younan, felt very pleased with himself. Today was the day; Dilawar would place the bombs in Cologne Cathedral and set them to detonate. Dilawar didn't know what the bombs contained and he didn't know that anyone would be hurt. He'd been told the only damage would be to the building; a painful destruction of one of their buildings which contained, according to the Christians, the body of Jesus Christ. How could he, their supposed Saviour, be in all the churches and cathedrals in the world? Mustafa didn't feel sorry that Dilawar would die too, quite horribly, in fact; he viewed Dilawar as a necessary tool to complete the job. He did wonder what Mashuum, Dilawar's grandad would think and if he would realise who'd made the bombs. Mustafa thought back to his meetings with Dilawar and decided that, apart from their chat in the room in the mosque, no one could link them together. Would Tawfeek show up once the bombs had gone off? Mustafa thought about that and felt sure that he would. Mustafa believed Tawfeek would be very happy with what he'd achieved in his absence, with the help and support of Nasir al Din Beshara, of course.

After eating his breakfast, Mustafa went down into the cellar and began to gather together the things he needed to make two more bombs. He was sticking to the schedule Tawfeek had given him, believing he was on a great mission.

Mustafa knew he had enough prepared ricin to make two more bombs; after which, he would have to process more of the castor beans he had stored. He had plenty of bottles, mason jars and filters so he wouldn't need to buy any more of those. Mustafa checked his watch once more and then began his vile work.

***

Mrs Williams was sitting in her office, sifting through her diary: a busy day, as usual on the horizon. She'd already been in her office for an hour, checking through the paperwork for the observations that were being done throughout the school for the whole week. The staff was nervous, but they knew the observations were to help them improve their performance in the classroom and keep the lessons on track so that they maintained their high end of year results. The observations were to help them. Except when they weren't! Mr Johnson, the CEO, was going to be part of the observation team. He was ultra-critical, rather than supportive, but if he wanted to observe lessons, what could she say but okay? Have to be on my best game too, Mrs Williams was thinking.

The phone rang and Mrs Williams picked it up.

"Who is it?"

"Mr Lodi, Dilawar Lodi's dad."

"Okay, put him through."

"Good morning, Mr Lodi. What can I do for you?"

Mrs Williams listened intently to what was being said.

"Not sure what the problem is, Mr Lodi. Isn't Dilawar away on the trip?"

Mrs Williams was struggling to keep up with the

conversation as Mr Lodi seemed very agitated and upset.

"Not sure I understand, Mr Lodi. Please take your time. Mr Lodi, are you there?"

"I'm sorry, Mrs Williams. It's Anna Lodi, Dilawar's step mum."

"Oh! Is there a problem?"

"We're not really sure. It's a long story, but the crux of it is we can't contact Dilawar and we think something's wrong."

Before Anna could continue, Mrs Williams butted in.

"I'm sure he's having such a wonderful time that he's forgotten to phone. Boys are like that. He'll be home late tomorrow and you'll be able to sort it out then," stated Mrs Williams, believing that would be the solution.

"I'm afraid that's not good enough. We're not sure if Dilawar is in trouble. He'd been staying with his grandad before he went away so we phoned his grandad to see if he knew anything. He didn't, but he was going to phone Dilawar himself and ask him, and then phone us back. When his grandad didn't phone back, we phoned him, but got no reply. In the end, we asked his neighbour, who has a key for emergencies, if he'd go in and check if Dilawar's grandad was okay. His grandad wasn't there, he hadn't been to the mosque as he usually does every day and he's still not at home. We need to talk with Dilawar to see if his grandad did speak with him and what, if anything, he said he was going to do."

"Well, this is most... unusual. I can see it must be very worrying for you. I'll phone Mr Andrews, the teacher who's in charge of the trip and get him to make sure Dilawar phones you. Can I have your number? If there's something wrong with Dilawar's phone so he just hasn't been able to phone you, I'll ask Mr Andrews to phone and let you know that was the reason he's been unavailable. I'm sure there's a rational explanation. I can't believe Dilawar's involved in anything bad as he's such a kind and conscientious young man."

"Thank you, Mrs Williams. We appreciate your help. Our number is 07549 674831. Thank you very much."

"No problem. Good morning."

Mrs Williams put the phone down and had the most awful feeling of dread. She shook it off, picked up the phone again and phoned Mr Andrews.

***

Dilawar sat at the breakfast table feeling quite unwell. He had drunk some water, eaten some bread and some cheese, but his stomach was really queasy. Could stress make you feel this unwell?

"Dilawar, you okay?" asked Zaigham. "You don't look much better than yesterday. What's wrong with you?"

"I think I must have eaten something somewhere that hasn't agreed with me. I'll just be glad to be home."

"You don't have to go to the cathedral today if you're not feeling well. I bet Mr Andrews would let you stay here."

"No, I need to go."

"Need to go? What sort of Muslim are you if you need to go to a cathedral?" asked Zaigham, laughing.

Dilawar was aware he needed to be careful what he said here. He was on the verge of replying when he heard his name being called.

"Yes, Mr Andrews?"

"Over here, Dilawar. I need to talk with you."

Dilawar felt even more ill, if that was possible.

185

"I'm okay, Mr Andrews. Just feel a bit off colour."

"Sorry? What?" asked Mr Andrews.

"Nothing, Sir."

"I've just had a call from Mrs Williams. Your parents are worried because they've tried to phone you and are getting nothing; something about your grandad."

"My grandad? What about him. Is he ill?"

"Look, I don't know. Where's your phone now?"

"In my pocket."

"Take it out and let's have a look."

Dilawar took the phone out of his pocket, looked at it and realised it was turned off. He looked at Mr Andrews.

"Sorry, Sir, I turned it off when we went into the theme park and forgot to turn it back on. What a div."

Mr Andrews laughed. "No problem. Give them a call now. You can do it in the games room as there's no one there. We're away to the cathedral in half an hour."

"Okay, thanks, Sir."

Dilawar turned his phone on and was shocked to see 8 missed calls from his dad and a full mailbox. He went to voicemail and listened to the garbled messages his dad had left. He didn't know what to do. None of the messages mentioned his grandad. Had Mr Andrews got it wrong? Dilawar went into his contacts and pressed his dad's number. It was answered immediately.

"Dilawar, what the hell's going on?"

Dilawar was shocked at the tremor in his dad's voice.

"I'm okay, Dad, my phone was off. Is there something wrong with Jadd?"

There was silence for a few seconds before Qusay

answered.

"We don't know. We were worried about you so we called Jadd to see if he knew what was going on. He didn't, but he was going to phone you and get back to us. He hasn't. Did he phone you?"

"No, he didn't. My phone was off and I forgot to put it back on. When I did, I had lots of missed calls from you, but nothing from Jadd. Why were you worried about me?"

"It's a long story, Dilawar. We'll talk when you get home. Unless you've something you want to talk about now?"

Dilawar hesitated, but not for long.

"No, Dad. I'm okay. I'll just be glad to get back home. We'll talk then."

"Are you sure?"

"Yes. Look, I have to go to the cathedral now. If I can, I'll phone you again as soon as I get back. If not, I'll see you tomorrow when I get home."

Without giving his dad time to reply, he finished the call and turned off his phone again. He walked out of the games room, gave a wave to Mr Andrews and then a thumbs up and made his way up to his room to collect the small rucksack which held the bombs. Dilawar sighed, wishing for the day to be over so that he had accomplished his task and was getting ready to go home. He would complete the mission set for him and hoped that the Prophet would protect him.

**

In Teynham, Qusay put down phone and dropped heavily into a chair, wondering what was going on and not convinced that everything was okay with Dilawar. Roll on tomorrow, he thought.

Chapter Twenty-Nine

A ringing phone broke through Qusay's reverie. He jumped up and ran to it, almost dropping it in his haste.

"Qusay, it's me. I have some questions for you," stated Mashuum.

"I've got some for you, too, where the hell have you been? Do you know how worried —"

Mashuum cut him off midstream.

"I have been with the police."

"The police?" parroted Qusay, whose grasp of the situation was non-existent. Before he could say another word, Anna had entered the room.

"Is that Mashuum?" she asked.

Qusay seemed unable to form the words he needed. He dropped into the armchair, handing the phone over to Anna.

"Father, where have you been? We've been so worried?" she asked.

"Look, Anna, I can catch you up on that later; it's Dilawar we have to worry about."

"Dilawar? He's on the trip."

"I haven't time to go into everything now, but it is crucial that you tell me where, exactly, Dilawar is at the moment."

Anna didn't know what to do or say, but the haunted look in Qusay's eyes was enough to steady her. They couldn't do with both of them falling apart.

"I'll just go get the itinerary and come back. I'll only be a minute as it's on the door of the fridge. You do know he's home tomorrow, don't you?"

"With the help of the Prophet," muttered Mashuum. "It's today we need to worry about."

Anna dashed into the kitchen and returned with the itinerary. Scanning through the details she found the information she needed.

"He's in Cologne today. They're visiting Cologne Cathedral and then doing some sight-seeing in groups."

"Do you know where they're staying?"

"No. We were just told they'd be in suitable accommodation. The school will know I should think. Why do you need to know all this?"

"I can't explain now, but I will get back to you later; if you believe in anything, now's the time to pray."

The call ended abruptly, leaving Anna to try to unravel the conversation she'd just had with Mashuum.

***

Mr Andrews was at the head of the snake making its way to Cologne Cathedral. The high gothic architecture amid the reconstructed old town, with the filigree twin towers, dominated the skyline. No wonder it was called the Mount Everest of Cathedrals.

"We will have a guide for the tour and then you will have some time to look around yourselves," stated Mr Andrews. "If you haven't already, you need to turn your phones off now. It would be extremely disrespectful if you let them ring while you were in the cathedral. You're not allowed to eat in there either, but you can have water to drink, so do make sure you don't spill any. Remember, too, that in any holy building, you need an 'inside' voice. Anyone tell me what that is?"

The same red-haired boy at the front of the line replied, "Whispering or talking quietly, Sir."

"Exactly. Make sure you know where the toilets are because they're not always as obvious here as in other buildings. Any questions?"

No reply so the groups traipsed behind Mr Andrews into the cathedral where they were met by their guide. Their bags were given a cursory check to ensure they didn't contain any food. Dilawar had handed one of the Nalgene bottles to Zaigham and asked him to hold it for him before their bags were checked. Zaigham never had a water bottle because he couldn't be bothered to fill one and he begrudged buying bottled water.

"Why two bottles, Dilawar?" Zaigham asked.

"I'm a bit dehydrated after not feeling well. I wasn't sure they'd let me take two bottles in."

"Okay. No problem. I'll give you it back when we get in."

"Thanks."

Dilawar felt quite sick and frightened as his bag was checked. He was worried, too, that Zaigham might drop the bottle he'd given him or try to drink from it. He didn't know what else he could do. By the time they were all inside with bags checked, Dilawar was feeling quite ill. He felt relieved when he had the bottles back in his rucksack.

"Guten morgen," said the guide.

"Guten morgen," the boys replied.

"That's all the German I got," whispered Wayne.

"Me, too," Jimmy replied.

At a look from Mr Bradley, the boys fell silent.

The group walked behind the guide admiring the interior of the cathedral and trying to note down some of the facts they were being given. They knew they would need them for the presentations they'd have to do once back at school.

"Those towers are gigantic," whispered Alfie, gazing up at them awestruck.

"I know," replied Jimmy, "but I wonder why the North Tower is 157.38 cm and the South Tower 150.38 cm? You'd think they'd be the same, wouldn't you?"

"This cathedral is called the Kölner Dom in German. There are five hundred and thirty-three steps up to the Dom's South Tower, to the base of the steeple that dwarfed all buildings until the Eiffel Tower was built in France," stated the guide.

"Wow!" whispered Alfie. "So many steps... My legs hurt just thinking about walking them."

"The Kölner Dom was completed in 1880 and it was under construction for five hundred years," continued the guide.

"Perhaps that's why the towers are different sizes?"

"Why?" asked Dilawar.

"Maybe during the five hundred years, someone lost the tape measure so they had to guess the sizes."

Dilawar couldn't help but laugh at Zaigham's comments.

"You are such an idiot, Zaigham."

"What? It could have happened that way."

"Yeah, right," said Jimmy, rolling his eyes as only teenagers can.

The boys were overwhelmed by the size of the cathedral. The guide's description of the phalanx of pillars and arches supporting the lofty nave were discussed, with the boys wondering how it had been possible to make such an impressive structure without modern-day tools. They were shown the tracery balustrade of the Choir Chapel which they thought quite beautiful. However, they were even more dazzled by the Shrine of the Three Kings behind the main altar. It was a richly gilded sarcophagus said to hold the remains of the kings who followed the star to the stable in Bethlehem, where Jesus was born. As the group walked around the cathedral, they were totally engrossed in the art and the treasures which were packed inside.

"You don't believe in Jesus, do you, Dilawar?" asked Wayne.

"What do you mean?" replied Dilawar.

"You believe in something else, don't you?" Wayne continued, as if trying to jog his memory.

"In the religion of Islam, we recognise Jesus as a prophet and we also honour his mother, Mary, but we don't believe he was a saviour, or the Son of God?"

"What do you believe, then?" continued Wayne, seemingly unable to assimilate all the information he was being given.

"We believe in the Prophet. We believe he was given the prayers of our holy book by the Archangel; prayers that we say every day."

"So, you pray like Christians?" asked Jimmy, quite interested in what Dilawar was saying.

"We probably pray more than Christians. Our Salah, or prayers, should be said five times a day."

"More things the same with the two religions than I thought," added Jimmy.

"I suppose you're right," stated Dilawar.

The guide had stopped walking and talking and was now shaking hands with Mr Andrews, who was thanking him in German, much to the delight of the guide.

In a quiet voice, Mr Andrews told them that they had a few hours to explore the cathedral themselves and visit the gift shop inside. The other teachers would be in the cathedral, walking round and looking at whatever they had found the most interesting. A time was set for the boys to meet outside the gift shop. Mr Andrews reminded them that the teachers' phones were also turned off, so if they needed anything, they would have to approach one of the members of staff who were walking around inside the cathedral. The groups of boys went their separate ways inside the cathedral walking towards the aspect of the cathedral they found the most interesting.

Chapter Thirty

In London, Adrian Smythe was back in his office trying to put a plan of action together. He'd had two messages while he'd been away: one from Ali and one from Jo Jacobs.

"Hi, Ali, you left a message for me."

"Hi, Adrian, I'm so pleased to hear your voice."

Despite the seriousness of the situation they were all facing, Adrian couldn't help the warm feeling he got from hearing Ali say that. Then he was annoyed with himself for it.

"What can I do for you?" he replied, trying to keep his mind on track and wondering what the hell was wrong with him.

"The traffic on the FfF website is going mad. There are lots of messages for Tawfeek and it's obvious from the tone that people are getting anxious about his non-availability."

"That's not good. It may spark them to alter their plans. We think we've got information on where the bombs are to be planted and we're looking into that with some haste. Is there any way you can pretend to be Tawfeek on there and stall them?"

"You mean, make it look as if I'm sending the message from his IP address?" Ali asked, with a slight tremor in her voice, recognising that what she was being asked to do wasn't quite legal.

"That's exactly what I'm asking. We just need a bit more

time to stop, or at least try to stop, a catastrophe."

A brief pause and then Ali replied, "Okay." She continued, "From the usual tone of his texts, he doesn't sound like a very nice person. Would you agree with that?"

"Overweening attitude doesn't even touch on what he's like."

"Okay, Adrian. I'll keep the tone the same and just say I'm away, it's important, I will be in touch when I get back. I can make it look like it's from his IP address and I think it should be more than enough to settle them down."

"Perfect, Ali. Thanks."

Adrian put the phone down and it rang immediately.

"Hi, Jo, you left me a message. What you got?"

"We've had the facial recognition software running continuously, but not coming up with much. I've recently written some additional code which will try to match any of the faces coming out of the mosque with anything in the media so we added that to the search pattern."

"And?"

"We've got a match. One of the photos had an old man with a much younger one coming out of the mosque. The younger one is matched with a video on South East Today of boys from a school in Kent going on a trip."

"To Dunkirk and Cologne?" asked Adrian.

"How did you know?" asked an exasperated Jo.

"You've confirmed some information I've just been given. Looks like the bombs are going to be detonated in Cologne, probably Cologne Cathedral. The young man's called Dilawar Lodi; I'll text you his mobile number. Can you trace it?"

"Yes, if it's on. If it's switched off, more problematic.

You want me to try?"

"Yes, and keep trying. I've got Jeff calling the head of the school he attends in Teynham to get the mobile number of the teacher in charge. Jeff will text that number to you as soon as he has it. I need you to try to trace that too. Don't ring the teacher or Lodi yourself, phone me straight away and I'll decide how to play this. Okay?"

"Okay, Boss."

Without skipping a beat, Adrian texted the PM on the number she'd given him for urgent calls with the words: 'Need to Facetime immediately.' He had barely sent the text when his laptop beeped. Showtime!

"Well?"

No preliminaries then.

"We have a strong lead on the name and location of the bomber. It's a young man called Dilawar Lodi, who has some link to the Zakaria Masjd Mosque. He's on a school trip and currently in Cologne, probably Cologne Cathedral. We've lots of information about him and we believe the information to be accurate."

"What are you doing about it at this precise moment?" asked the PM.

"I've got someone trying to trace his phone; an operative getting the phone number of the teacher in charge of the trip who I will contact, and I have Porton Down on standby to transport vaccine for ricin to anywhere in Europe, at short notice."

"Okay. Not much else you can do at the moment, but keep me up to speed with what's going on. I'll now contact Chancellor Angela Merkel, and tell her we believe one of our young people has taken one, or possible two or more, bombs into her country and it looks like they're going to be detonated today in Cologne Cathedral. Should be an easy conversation that one!"

"Would you like me to contact my counterpart in Germany before you do that, or do you want to leave it to the Chancellor?"

The PM ran her hands across the sides of her head, stretching and grimacing as she did so.

"No. I think it best I let the Chancellor do that. I will, however, tell her that we have vaccine for the ricin and could get it to her immediately. Contact Porton Down and ensure they've got some packed up to be collected and despatched by helicopter to Cologne, as soon as they get a phone call from me or my Deputy."

"Will do, Ma'am."

***

Dilawar had 'escaped' from his group by saying he was going to the toilet and would then sit and wait for them by the gift shop. He went towards the toilets and the other boys went in the opposite direction. Dilawar was feeling quite sick and weak again so he was grateful when he found the toilets were empty. In the toilet, he threw up with some force and was retching for a couple of minutes. He hadn't realised stress could make you so ill. Or was it guilt about what he was going to do, he wondered? He ran the cold water tap and splashed water over his face. Even he could see how pale he was. Dilawar dabbed at his face with a paper towel, surprised to find that his forehead felt quite hot. Just one more day and I'll be home.

Coming out of the toilet area, Dilawar made the decision to head to the Shrine of the Three Kings. He walked slowly through the cathedral, admiring the beauty that it contained and feeling the peace of the place. Sitting down on a bench close by, he watched the look of awe and wonder on the people who passed him as they gazed at the many treasures and pieces of art before them: many colours of skin and many cultures. Dilawar's face did not reflect the beauty of the cathedral; it reflected his inner turmoil. He was struggling with what he was supposed to do. Although Mustafa Younin had told Dilawar that only the fabric of the building would be affected, Dilawar was beginning to have doubts. In his heart, he knew he shouldn't plant the bombs and set them ready for detonation to destroy any part of the beautiful building in which he was sitting. He thought of Jadd and how he would react when he heard what Dilawar had done. In his innocence, Dilawar had thought he could complete the mission he'd been set and then return home. It was only now beginning to dawn on him what a heinous act it would be and how the repercussions would reflect the act. What was he to do?

Tears ran rivers down his face as he struggled to work out what to do. Should he phone Jadd? He knew phones had to be off in the cathedral but, if he went back to the toilets and turned his on, who would know? He could then phone Jadd; he would know what to do. Dilawar wondered if it was his dad he should phone, rather than Jadd. He thought back to the conversation he'd had with his dad before leaving for the cathedral. He couldn't quite remember what had been said but, now he thought back, his dad was obviously worried that something was wrong. What did he know, Dilawar wondered? And how did he know? The urge to vomit again was so strong; Dilawar had to almost run back to the toilets. Fierce vomiting and retching left him feeling weak and dizzy. Dilawar turned his phone on and then just sat on the floor looking at the screen. He had trouble focussing. Dilawar struggled to his feet and went back into a toilet cubicle. He locked the door, put the lid down on the toilet seat and sat on it. Dilawar tried once more to focus on the screen of his phone; suddenly, he had such a headache that it seemed to split his skull in two, and then, blackness as he slipped into oblivion.

Chapter Thirty-One

"You're sure?" Adrian asked, unable to keep the excitement out of his voice.

"I wouldn't call you if I wasn't," replied Jo Jacobs, with just a touch of annoyance in her voice.

We're all too tired, thought Adrian, recognising the tiredness behind the annoyance.

"Sorry, Jo, I wasn't doubting you. I couldn't believe you could trace him so fast."

"Apology accepted. Lodi's phone was off when I first tried to trace it, but it came on about ten minutes ago. He's in Cologne Cathedral, as you thought. I haven't been able to trace the teacher's phone because that's still off, but I'll continue to try."

"Brilliant work. I'll leave you with that while I get back on to the PM."

"I'll let you know as soon as I have anything else."

"Great."

He sent another text to the PM, followed by the beep of his laptop.

"Well?"

Adrian looked at the PM's face and could see the worry etched on it.

"We've traced Lodi's phone to Cologne Cathedral, but haven't been able to trace the teacher's phone yet, but I've got my best tech still trying. When we get the number, I will ring him. As the Germans haven't got any vaccine against ricin at the moment, I think it best that a hazmat team go into the cathedral. Then, they at least will have some protection against the ricin. Hopefully, they'll be able to find Lodi or the bombs or, better still, Lodi and the bombs. People inside would have to be moved out of the cathedral and transported to a containment site somewhere. The team won't be able to keep the people inside in case the bombs are primed to go off. They also can't mix people from inside the cathedral with the general public in case they're infected. The scientists at Porton Down have two lots of vaccine because the strain of ricin that we've got is not the same as the one we've had before. It's unstable, which is another complication. We don't know if this unstable ricin will take effect immediately on release, if it can be passed on by contact or even the full extent of its ingestion."

"I'll get on to the Chancellor and tell her the 'good' news. If she needs our help, she can have it, but she will probably deal with it herself. I'll arrange for the vaccines to be transported immediately, once she tells me where the helicopter will be able to land."

"Franz Sneider, my counterpart in Germany, is first class so I'm sure he's already on top of the situation. I'll phone him and give him the mobile number of Lodi and of the teacher, if you think that's appropriate?"

"Okay. I think that's a good idea. Anything else?"

"What shall I do about Lodi's family? They've been worried about his behaviour, but didn't envisage anything like this. His grandfather, to whom he's really close, has been a great help to us in this and given total support."

"Give them as much information as you think they need,

but ensure they don't start talking about all this to anyone. We don't want the media on this and turning it into a circus. We need to have it sewn up before news leaks out."

"Okay, Ma'am."

***

Every country has an emergency plan that should cover all and every conceivable emergency; Germany was no exception. Over time, their plans had evolved to cover emerging technologies that could be used to hurt or destroy: chemical and nuclear attacks, terrorist attacks and much, much more; a constantly changing plan to reflect the constantly changing world they inhabited. In some countries, a threat such as that facing Germany would have been met by a chaotic response. Not so in Germany. The threat there was dealt with by the Chancellor and her security staff with speed, precision and determination to avert what they now knew would be a catastrophe of immense proportions.

The tech staff went into immediate action, accessing the traffic light system to stop vehicles entering into the vicinity of the cathedral. Those that were currently near to the cathedral were diverted to what was felt to be a safe distance away from it. Roadside signs showed road closures for the rest of the day and diverted routes were indicated. No reason was given for the road closures. Two response teams were sent out: one to control the traffic on the roads and move traffic out of the area as quickly as possible and one team to surround the cathedral, ensuring no one left the building. Both teams were armed; two helicopters were in the air to monitor the situation and control any build up of traffic or people.

On arrival at the cathedral, the commander of the team went in the main entrance and asked to speak to the security chief. The security men on the door were rather surprised to see an armed response officer asking for their chief, but they complied with his request and buzzed their chief. Within minutes, the chief had arrived and was deep in conversation with the commander; the chief's face becoming paler and paler as the conversation continued. With a nod of heads and a handshake, the conversation was ended. The commander went back outside and the chief turned to his men.

"We have a… situation," he began. "There's a strong possibility we have a bomber inside the cathedral." At this comment, there was a communal gasp from his men. He continued, "We have to lock everyone inside, including ourselves, and make sure no one leaves the building."

"What about the side doors?" asked Helmut, one of the younger guards.

"All of them," replied the chief, glancing around at his men. "The response team outside have surrounded the cathedral and will stay there until ordered to leave."

"Why aren't they going in to look for the bomber?" Helmut asked.

The chief paused wondering how much he should tell them. If they had to stay locked inside the cathedral, he decided they should know the extent of the problem.

"They think the bomber may have ricin in the bombs that will be dispersed into the atmosphere when the bombs explode. A hazmat team is on its way and should be here very soon."

"Why would he have rice inside the bombs and what's a hazmat team?" enquired Helmut.

"Not rice, ricin — which is a chemical agent — and a hazmat team is one that's wearing protection against hazardous materials."

"Like ricin?"

"Yes."

"Helmut's face was now very pale and he looked like he might faint. "Oh my God! Oh my God!"

"Get a hold of yourself, Helmut. We've got to stay calm and do our job," replied the chief, giving Helmut's shoulders a shake.

"But… But what about us? We need to leave. We should get out. Now!" Helmut's voice rose with every word and his feet seemed to be making their own way to the front entrance.

A pull on his arm from the chief made him stop in his tracks. Putting his face up to Helmut's the chief continued, "We can't leave. The response team won't allow us to leave. We may already be infected; they don't know. Now get back to your post and do your job," the last few words were said in a very harsh tone as the chief pushed Helmut back towards the desk.

The silence was deafening. Every face a pale canvas etched with fear. Every person was trying to stand up straight and be counted. The chief picked up the walkie talkie from the desk and proceeded to talk to all his members of staff in the building. The message was that they had a 'situation' and that everyone was to stay inside the building until they were told otherwise. That message given, the chief made his way into the cathedral hoping that his calm presence would allay any fears or worries his staff may have until the relevant people had arrived to take charge. He hoped that wouldn't be long.

Outside the cathedral, the response team was on full alert.

People wishing to go into the cathedral were turned away and directed to other places they might like to see at the other side of Cologne. Buildings close to the cathedral were not evacuated at this stage as it was felt that would cause widespread panic. When the hazmat team arrived, it would be their call whether to evacuate them or not, once they'd assessed the situation. Security fences were put around the cathedral so no one could slip into the building — or out of it. What they had to do now was the hardest thing. Wait.

Chapter Thirty-Two

Entering the interview room, Adrian was shocked to see the change in Mashuum Lodi. He seemed to have shrunk in size and his ashen face reflected his distress.

"You have news?" asked Mashuum.

"I have, but it's not good I'm afraid," replied Adrian, pausing for a few seconds. "I didn't expect to find you still here as I gave instructions for you to be released," he continued.

"I stayed to pray because I needed the comfort of the Prophet to show me what I had to do to help."

"And what's that?" Adrian asked, intrigued despite himself.

"I've made a list of everyone with whom I know my grandson had contact when we went to the mosque. It's not a huge list and I may have missed some, but I think it's quite accurate."

Mashuum handed the list to Adrian who couldn't help, but admire the beautiful handwriting script that flowed on the cheap paper. One name immediately leapt out at him: Abdul-Azeem Tawfeek. Adrian glanced up to see Mashuum's expectant gaze.

"What contact did your grandson have with Abdul-Azeem Tawfeek?"

"Dilawar attended his talks whenever he visited and he

admired him, I think. Why did you focus on that name straight away?"

Adrian didn't know how much to tell Mashuum, so he hesitated.

"Do one thing for me first. Tick the names on this list of people who also attended Tawfeek's talks?" asked Adrian, as he passed the list back to Mashuum.

Mashuum scrolled down the list, marking four ticks on the paper. He then handed the list back to Adrian, without passing comment. Sitting back in the chair, Mashuum waited for Adrian to scan the ticks he'd made and put the list down on the table.

"What I tell you now is not to be passed on to your son, until I tell you it's okay to do so. Do you agree to that?"

"Why can't I tell Qusay, he's beside himself with worry?"

"I'm sure he is but, trust me, if you don't agree to that condition, I can't tell you anything. I'm very grateful that you've stayed to help us, despite your obvious worry and distress, and what you've given me now is very important. However, I'm not allowed to tell you anything without your agreement not to pass on anything at the moment. I'm sorry."

Mashuum took a minute and then he nodded his agreement.

"We believe Tawfeek is a key player in the radicalisation of young men in your mosque. We believe your grandson has been manipulated into taking one or two bombs with him on his school trip. He'll plant them and set them to detonate."

Mashuum was on his feet, walking around the room, tugging at his beard and shaking his head from side to side.

"No! No! Dilawar is a good boy. He wouldn't do this. He wouldn't!"

Adrian waited until Mashuum had stopped pacing and was back sitting on the chair. Mashuum looked at him, eyes pleading.

"There's worse to come?" asked Mashuum, his words unsteady.

"I'm afraid so. The bombs contain a chemical agent that will be dispersed when the bombs are detonated, killing large numbers of people. We don't think your grandson knows about the chemical agent and that, in all possibility, he too will be killed."

"How do you know all this?" Mashuum asked.

"This isn't the first time Tawfeek's been involved in this sort of thing. He engages young men and then, in some way, tricks them into doing his dirty work. He's not doing it on his own, but is part of a network of Muslims whose sole aim is to kill Christians or non-Muslims."

"But this is not what Islam is about. The Prophet never told Muslims to kill. He gave us exquisite prayers and a way of life that was good and holy. To us Muslims, Jesus Christ is recognised as a prophet and his mother, Mary, is respected. I don't understand all this hate," Mashuum stated, confusion evident in his tone of voice.

Again, Adrian waited for Mashuum to calm down, the silence in the room broken only by Mashuum grinding his teeth as he gazed at the floor, lost in his troubled thoughts. After a few minutes, Mashuum sat up straight in the chair and looked directly at Adrian.

"You need to tell me the rest now. I'm ready."

"We've traced your grandson to Cologne Cathedral. The building is sealed off and secure at the moment. When the appropriate team arrives, they will go into the cathedral, find your grandson and the bombs and do whatever they need to do to make the situation safe."

Mashuum didn't reply. He looked around the room, orientated himself and fell onto his knees to pray. Adrian got up and walked quietly out of the room. He told the guard to leave Mashuum where he was while he was praying then to escort him back to his cell. The door to the cell was not to be locked as Mashuum was no longer in custody; he was helping them. Adrian walked away fighting the despair he often felt when innocents were being hurt.

***

In his cellar, Mustafa Younan was putting the finishing touches to his next two bombs, thinking how great it was that he could do the things he liked doing and get credit for them. Life was good. His burner phone pinged and he was feeling very happy, expecting it to be Dilawar Lodi letting him know the bombs had been planted and set to go off as they'd planned. He was startled on two accounts: the text was from Nasir al Din Beshara and the only word on the screen was 'flee'.

Frozen with fear, Mustafa couldn't think what he should do. The phone pinged again. He was so frightened he could barely push the button to light up the screen of his phone, another message from Beshara: one word again, but this time it said, 'NOW!!'

"Prophet, help me!" he shouted, as he dropped the phone, cracking the screen.

It took Mustafa a few minutes to calm himself, and then he had to think. You should always have an escape plan, he'd been told. He didn't have one. Not as clever as he thought.

After much muttering and thinking, jotting notes down, then crossing them out, he had a plan. He'd go visit some relatives in Bradford for a few months until things calmed down. He could still get the payment for his lockup to the owner, so the castor beans and the equipment would be safe for as long as he could make the payments. Mustafa had lots of cousins in Bradford so getting some cash-in-hand work wouldn't be a problem. He'd leave a note for his parents telling them he needed some space and was going travelling to find himself. He'd heard someone else say that before and thought at the time it sounded pretty lame, but his parents would accept it. What to do with the bombs? He'd have to think about that while he was getting his things together. Mustafa really didn't want to take them with him because he had no intention of getting involved in the planting and detonation. Must be something else he could do? He'd have to think about it.

***

Alan Edwards was not a happy man. His team had gone to pick up Nasir al Din Beshara at his house, only to find he wasn't there. His car was there, as was his wife, son and two daughters, but no Beshara. His wife would not talk with them, but his son was happy to do so. According to him, his father had been away for a few weeks. His son had no idea where he was or when he was coming back. The bonnet of the car in the drive was still warm, but when asked who'd been driving it, the son said that he had, a huge smile on his face. The team had no alternative, but to leave. Adrian was not happy either when Alan phoned to let him know Beshara had flown the coop, but there was nothing they could do other than put a hold on his passport, which Adrian did.

Adrian informed Alan that he'd scanned and emailed a list to him of people he'd been told had had dealings with Abdul-Azeem Tawfeek. The people were to be picked up and taken in for questioning about their dealings with Tawfeek, once their backgrounds had been checked. Alan apologised again to Adrian for the failure of his team to pick-up Beshara but Adrian said that you can't win them all. He knew Alan's team did a great job and none of them needed to feel guilty if the people thought to be criminals were also clever and, sometimes, escaped their clutches. Perhaps the backgrounds of the people on the list might be an indicator of the depth of their involvement with Tawfeek?

Chapter Thirty-Three

Sitting at the head of the conference table in her office, Mrs Williams, the head of Teynham School, was doing her best to keep eye contact with Mr Johnson, the Chief Executive of the Winning Ways Trust, who sat opposite her. She knew he was angry, or anxious, or both, because she could see the movement of one of his legs as it jiggled up and down under the table. She was momentarily distracted from what he was saying; she wondered if he was on the spectrum — a high achieving person with autism — as so many 'clever' people were. She was brought back to her senses by a sudden change in his tone as he got up from the table and began to pace.

"Well?" he asked.

As she hadn't been paying attention and was, at that very moment, thinking that he was wearing very ugly, cumbersome shoes, her body jerked to attention.

"Sorry, could you repeat the question?"

If looks could kill, was the appropriate phrase, as he began to repeat his earlier question.

"What exactly do we know about what's happening in Cologne?" he asked, annunciating each word,

"Not much. Dilawar Lodi's parents phoned because they hadn't heard from him. His behaviour before he went on the trip had been a bit worrying for them, so they wanted to make sure he was okay. I reassured them as best I could and said I'd contact Mr Andrews and get him to sort the matter out. As far as I know, that's what happened. The boy must have phoned his parents because I heard nothing else."

"That's not unusual, boys often forget to phone."

"True, but I've just had a call from the police asking for the phone number of the teacher in charge of the trip. I asked them why and they said they couldn't comment, but needed the number immediately. I was instructed not to phone him myself, not to tell anyone about their call and told that they'd get back to me later to update me. I mentioned that we were part of the trust and that you, the Chief Executive, was here at the moment and I asked if I could tell you. They said I could, but with the same instructions that you were not to talk to anyone about this matter."

"Did you verify that they were actually the police, or worse, some journalist trying to get information?"

Of course. With all the policies we have to have, the contact number should we need to inform the police of anything, was in the folder. The officer I spoke with checked with the senior in the department and verified we were to give the police, who'd contacted us, the information they needed," replied Mrs Williams.

"Okay, I suppose. What's this boy, Dilawar Lodi, like?"

Mrs Williams took a minute to gather her thoughts before she spoke.

"He's a good lad, a conscientious student, perhaps a bit withdrawn."

"What do you mean by 'withdrawn'?" asked Mr Johnson, an edge to his voice.

"Well, he has a small group of friends, but he doesn't socialise very much. I think he struggles with the behaviour of

213

some of the children here."

"What do you mean; what behaviour?" his tone sounding like a rebuke.

"Dilawar talks a lot about his grandad to whom he's very close. He loves going to the mosque with him and, from what his teachers have said, Dilawar has a very good grasp of Islam and ways people should behave, so children who are a bit 'over the top' with their behaviour and dress make him feel uncomfortable."

"I see," came the curt reply.

Mr Johnson continued to pace for a couple of minutes, before he spoke again.

"Okay. I'm going back to my base office; keep me informed of any developments, immediately!"

"I will, of course," replied Mrs Williams, wondering if he really did see. And see what?

You couldn't call him Mr Wooden if you saw him now, she thought, remembering an overheard conversation on the phone between Gwen Masters and Jenny Evans of South East Today, on the day the boys went on the trip.

***

Jo Jacobs was doing a background check on the four names on Mashuum Lodi's list. The first two names had innocuous backgrounds, as far as she could tell. The third, however, looked more interesting. Qualifications in science and recent attendance at university where he gained a BSc. Jo wanted to check out the background of the fourth before she passed on any relevant information to Alan Edwards in Leeds, unwilling to jump at the first positive.

"Got any spare time, Ali," Jo asked.

"You've got another job for me?"

"I have. I thought you might be up for it."

"I'm intrigued. I'm still monitoring the FfF website, but I'll be alerted if anything with the relevant search parameters pops up. Give me the gen and I'll see what I can do," replied Ali.

"Brilliant! I've been given a list of people who had contact with our prospective bomber and who also attended talks by Tawfeek. Of the four names on the list, one is jumping out at me. However, I need to do the same background check on the fourth name before I can move the investigation on."

"Okay. What's the possible link and what's the name?"

"Link is a science degree and the name's Mustafa Younan. I know you were looking for establishments where equipment had been stolen, so this might tie in with that. Then again, it might not, but it's worth investigating further. I'm sending all the information I've got on him over to you now. I'll need an hour on what I'm doing at the moment, so will get back to you after that, unless you need to contact me sooner because you've got something."

"Sounds like a good plan," stated Alli, as she put the phone down.

"What does?" asked Dan, as he walked into the room.

"You're like that game where you have to keep bashing the head of the animal, but it keeps popping up. Where've you been?"

"I popped out to buy some kit for my next fishing trip to Spain, and then I popped back in."

"Very funny! Thought you weren't going away for a while?"

"I wasn't, but the lure of the barbel is too strong; it's calling me," replied Dan, in his most theatrical voice, arm across his forehead in a dramatic pose.

"Oh, please! Barbel? What happened to your first love, carp?"

"Been there, done that."

"I can't keep up with you. Anyway, I've got to get on with this as I'm on a deadline."

"Okay, give me a shout if you need anything: Jasmine tea, Sandwich, Cake, Chocolate?" offered Dan, as he was walking out of the room.

Ali seriously considered the offer of chocolate, but decided not to be tempted. She turned instead to the task in hand.

***

"I've had a text," stated Qusay Lodi.

"From who?" Anna asked.

"My dad."

"Your dad? You must have got it wrong, Q, your dad doesn't text."

Qusay pushed the phone towards her.

"Here!" Qusay, said, pointing to the message. "I don't get it. What on earth's going on?"

Anna looked again at the message. All it said was that Mashuum was safe and would get back to them later. She decided to phone him to see if she could find out what was going on. The phone was switched off.

Chapter Thirty-Four

The hazmat team had arrived at the cathedral and, within a very short space of time, a large white tent had been set up and their equipment put inside it. The commander of the security team guarding the exterior of the cathedral was in deep conversation with the team's boss, HZ1. Once the conversation was finished, the commander returned to his post and the team boss to the tent where his team was waiting for further instructions.

"We've no more information than what we were given before we set off. The vaccine's on its way, but we can't wait any longer, hence our hazmat suits. As far as we know, what we're wearing should protect us. However, we believe the ricin in the bombs is a variant, so we're not sure of its stability," stated HZ1.

"Happy days are here again," sang Jeff, the second in command, trying to lighten the mood.

The team didn't use their names outside of the unit, referring only to themselves by their HZ number, for security reasons. None of the team questioned that; people in their line of work were very conscious of their safety and that of their families. Should a terrorist be able to find out where they lived, given what they do, the terrorist would have no compunction in making a direct attack on them and their families; better safe than sorry.

On the table in the tent was a plan of the interior of the cathedral. HZ1 allocated teams of three to each section. Each team was to go to their area, search and secure it. That meant moving any visitors to what was felt to be a safe spot. Well, as safe as it could be under the circumstances. If any bombs were found, HZ1 was to be informed immediately, using the walkie talkies. The team then had to wait until he arrived at their location. No phones were to be used. Phones had sometimes been used to detonate bombs; therefore, again, the 'better safe than sorry' adage was applied. Whichever team came upon Mr Andrews and the boys from Teynham School, they were to move the group close to the entrance and keep them there until HZ1 arrived. Obviously, the team would need to check that all the boys were there, including Dilawar Lodi, but caution was needed in case he detonated the bombs when he realised he'd been made, if he hadn't already planted them.

"Any questions?" asked HZ1.

"What if we find small groups of boys from the school, but no teachers?" asked HZ5.

"You'll still have to move them close to the entrance and leave at least one member of the team with them," HZ1 replied.

No more was said. The team split into their respective trios and followed HZ1 as he walked into the cathedral. The security team just inside the cathedral gave shocked glances as the group of white-suited men entered and made their way to the interior. HZ1 watched as each trio set off to their allocated space. A few heads turned as they entered and there was more than one face that showed fear.

Each small team worked methodically in their search for the bombs. People were herded into small groups, their

218

questions left unanswered, as there was no time for pleasantries when a bomb could possibly be detonated at any time. Mr Andrews and Mr Malik were found in front of the Shrine of the Three Kings discussing the richly gilded sarcophagus and the possibility that the remains of the three kings were actually enclosed. DNA testing was being suggested as a way to confirm the findings were what they were said to be. Hearing an unusual rustling, Mr Andrews turned around and gave a start at what he saw: a shape in a large white suit, eyes looking through a screen.

"What the…"

Before he could say more, a voice said, "Name please?"

Both men replied at the same time," Michael Andrews; Javid Malik."

"From Teynham School in Kent?"

Both men nodded their heads.

"Come with me."

Obediently, they followed, still in shock, but wondering what was going on? When they arrived at what obviously was their destination by the entrance to the cathedral, they found some of the boys from the trip waiting, looking quite frightened.

"Sir, Sir, what's going on?" asked two of the boys at the same time.

Mr Andrews shrugged his shoulders and was going to reply, but was stopped by the man — he presumed it was a man in the suit because of the size — who'd found them at the Shrine of the Three Kings. He took Mr Andrews to one side and began to question him about the number of boys on the trip and how many had come to the cathedral with him.

"What's this all about? Surely you can tell me that?"

asked Mr Andrews.

The man in the white suit shook his head and continued as if Mr Andrews hadn't spoken.

"There are fifteen boys here, where are the other nine?"

Mr Andrews turned to the group of boys and counted them.

"We have five groups; three of them are here and two groups — one of five boys and one of four — are in the cathedral somewhere. They were given a time to be back here and there's twenty minutes before their time's up in the cathedral."

"Thank you. Is Dilawar Lodi in this group of fifteen?"

"Dilawar?" asked Mr Andrews, turning to the group. "No, why?"

The man didn't reply, but turned when he heard the walkie talkie on his belt buzzing.

The team tasked to check the toilets and the area around the toilets had found one of them locked. HZ4 had gone into the cubicle next to the one that was locked, climbed, with some difficulty, onto the toilet seat, and peered over. The young man inside was sitting on the toilet seat, slumped to the side, and looked to be unconscious. He was clutching a rucksack and a phone was on the floor. The team secured the area, informed HZ1 and waited. He was with them within minutes, did exactly the same thing HZ4 had done and then decided to see if he could make contact.

"Dilawar, Dilawar Lodi?" he shouted over the top of the cubicle. No response.

"Dilawar, we're here to help you." There was still no response.

As the team was all wearing hazmat suits, they couldn't get the door of the toilet open. HZ4 went back to the guards at the entrance and asked for a screwdriver. Moving as quickly as he could, he took the flat head screwdriver into the toilet area. The door was soon opened with it and it was clear that Dilawar was unconscious. What wasn't clear was if he still had the bombs. So far, none had been found in the cathedral, so there was every chance they were still in the rucksack which was clasped to Dilawar's chest. There was going to have to be some manoeuvring. HZ1 indicated that all the men should leave the toilet area, which they did. He followed them out. HZ2 was tasked with phoning HQ to update them on the current situation, arranging with them an ambulance with suitably-suited medical staff to be sent, to take Dilawar to a hospital, or wherever they needed to take him. Isolation was necessary until they could find out if he was just ill or if it was a reaction to the ricin. In the meantime, HZ1 and HZ3 were going to work together to try to remove the rucksack from Dilawar's arms and find out if it contained a bomb or bombs. The other teams were now moving all the visitors further away from the toilet areas. Coaches were on their way to take all of them to a place of safety where they could be examined and assessed and, hopefully, vaccinated. They wouldn't be happy but that's the way it had to be.

HZ3 went back out to the tent to collect the lead container into which they'd put the bombs, if the bombs were still in the rucksack and if they were able to get them out. The worry was that the bombs could be booby-trapped to detonate if someone interfered with them. If he could, HZ3 would have crossed all of his fingers and all of his toes, hoping that weren't the case. However, the hazmat suit meant that wasn't possible. For some reason, he couldn't get the words of the song HZ2 had sung in the tent out of his head, finding himself humming it as he went back to the toilet area. He really hoped happy days were here again.

Chapter Thirty-Five

"Ali? Ali? You okay?" shouted Dan as he crossed the room to where Ali was standing immobile, in an unusual position. He'd left two hours before to go and buy some equipment for his next trip to Spain. She'd been fine then.

"What? Who?" replied Ali, changing her posture as she spoke.

"Are you okay?" asked Dan again.

"Why wouldn't I be?"

Dan thought for a minute, wondering how he could put into words what he'd just seen. He decided he couldn't, so adopted the pose that Ali had been in when he entered the room — the same eyes-closed, body crouching pose.

Ali stared at him for the briefest of moments before laughter erupted from her slim form and threatened to overwhelm her. Dan, even more confused, could only stand and watch until the bubbling mass that was Ali, had returned to some sense of normality.

"I never knew," she offered.

"Never knew what?" questioned Dan.

"That when you're standing like a tree in tai chi, you actually look as if you're constipated, but without the troubled look that comes with constipation." Again, she erupted into laughter.

Dan, now in an upright position and smiling, replied," I

should have known it was something to do with your kung fu class. I thought you were having some sort of… sort of turn."

Dan always joked that the tai chi class was kung fu, or Chinese line dancing, but Ali refused to take the bait this time.

"I thought you were on the case for Adrian trying to track down bombers and the like."

"I am, but the software I was using wasn't quite up to the task so I updated it and, while it was running, I was getting very uptight wondering if I'd get the hit soon enough. Standing like a tree to control my breathing and calm me down seemed to be the answer."

"Okay, but I thought you were tracking facial recognition and were well on it?"

"I was and I got a hit that confirmed who the bomber is, then Super Techie asked me to track down some information which should, we hope, identify the bomb maker."

"So that's why the 'soon enough'; you're worried the bomber might have made even more bombs to be planted somewhere else?"

"You're so clever. That's exactly why the hurry."

"I won't hold you up then, Ali, but I could get you some sustenance, perhaps? I just happen to have brought you some, rather delicious, triple chocolate gateau."

"Wow! I could really murder a piece of that."

"Okay, be back in ten with a slice of cake and a coffee from the machine."

"Perfect." Not for the first time, Ali wondered what she'd do without Dan to look after her. Just the thought gave her that cold feeling you get when you consider the loss of someone so dear to you: a loss that would leave you feeling less than whole. Doesn't bear thinking about, she thought. Too scary!

She was distracted from her thoughts by a ping from her laptop. She wasn't the first one this day to hope she could cross all of her fingers and all of her toes hoping that would bring her good luck.

***

In Cologne Cathedral, HZ1 and HZ3 were still in the toilet area, trying to work out how best to do what they had to do. Neither of them were small men and, in their hazmat suits, they were even larger. Getting the rucksack from Lodi's arms in the toilet cubicle, without setting off the bombs if they were still inside, was the major hurdle. Lodi might resist and detonate. They needed both of them to do that one task together so that one could restrain, if necessary, while the other removed the bag. Time was moving on and they didn't seem to be.

HZ3 was the most experienced with bombs, so he was going to have to remove the bag and take it out of the cubicle, while HZ1 did the rest. Before they moved in, HZ3 had gone into the next cubicle, reached under the bottom of it and retrieved Lodi's phone, very carefully. He didn't press any switches or buttons because he didn't know if the bombs were to be detonated by phone, as often happened. He walked outside the toilet area, handed the phone to HZ2, spoke quietly to him and then walked back into the toilet area.

"Dilawar? Dilawar Lodi? We're here to help you. Can you speak?" asked HZ1.

No response. No movement. Lodi's body was still crouched over.

"Let's get on with it," whispered HZ1.

HZ3 stepped forward and moved into a crouching

position. He scanned the area around the bag: nothing visible — no wires. He turned his head slightly to indicate that HZ1 was to move into position, which he did, almost flattened against the left side of the cubicle. Not much room to move. HZ3 leaned in and put one hand gently on the outside of the front of the rucksack. Still, there was no response from Lodi. A nod again from HZ3. HZ1 moved forward very slightly until he could rest his fingers on Lodi's neck, his pulse was very faint and erratic. He moved his hand down onto Lodi's shoulder, putting no pressure on it at all, but ready to do so if needed. Each man seemed to be holding their breath in, conscious that things could change in the blink of an eye. They'd been in such situations before and lived to tell the tale.

Very gently, HZ3 put his hands on top of the rucksack and cautiously moved his hands down the sides, searching for the zip. It was quite close to the bottom of the left side. Glancing up at Lodi's face, he was checking that nothing had changed. HZ1 was struggling with the position he was in. There was so little space; he couldn't put any pressure on so he was in imminent danger of going into cramp. He knew to move sharply could bring a catastrophic result so he was grinding his teeth to try to remain focussed.

HZ1 lifted Lodi's arm away from the rucksack, moving it locked in the clasping shape as gently as he could. HZ3 moved in to lift the other arm away, but was met with some resistance; it was as if Lodi's arm was in rigor. He glanced up at HZ1 who was just about maintaining his position, cramp an advancing enemy. HZ3 could have broken Lodi's arm and moved the rucksack away quickly and no one would have blamed him because of the possibility of detonation. He was not that man. He had no idea why Lodi had wanted to plant bombs to kill people and he would not allow himself to be the judge of this young man's actions by treating him differently. A person in a dangerous situation is just that, nothing more.

HZ3 moved towards Lodi and whispered quietly into his ear.

"I'll take the rucksack, Dilawar. You can let it go now."

He whispered this, three times, and was just about to give up hope, when a gentle sigh escaped from the young man's lips and his body seemed to sag even more in the space.

Taking a chance, HZ3 quickly moved the slightly more relaxed arm away and moved the rucksack to his own chest. Struggling to his feet, he then moved out of the cubicle, giving HZ1 the space to check Lodi's vitals.

"Not good," muttered HZ1.

The even trickier bit was now to come. HZ3 could drop the rucksack into the lead container and take it outside. However, he still wasn't sure that the bombs were still inside.

"Going to next phase," he shouted to HZ1.

"Picking up the lead container, HZ3 moved to the end of the toilet area, into the larger disabled toilet. He opened the container and put it on the changing mat which was about waist level in the cubicle. The moment of truth. Gingerly, HZ3 unzipped the rucksack. Inside were two Nalgene water bottles. He lifted one up and examined it. He hated this part of his job because if the bomb was booby trapped, this is when it could go off. However, he had to check because he needed to know. He saw an efficient and simple detonation mechanism on the bomb and, he supposed, the fluid inside was the ricin. He put both bottles carefully into the lead container and sealed it. They still weren't safe, but they were safe enough to be moved to a place where they could be defused and their evil contents removed in a safe environment.

Chapter Thirty-Six

"That's that then," muttered Jo Jacobs to herself, as she finished her search of the fourth name on the list she'd been given. She hadn't found any link which would incriminate the man.

"Hi, Ali," she said but, in return, all she could hear was the rustling of paper.

"Ali, you there?" she continued.

"Sorry. Give me a minute." There was more shuffling of paper.

Jo tapped on the desk, impatience threatening to overwhelm her. She knew they were close, but she also knew they needed to be closer.

"Sorry, Super T, but I was just putting it all together."

"Putting what together, Ali?"

"Sorry. Just need a minute to catch my breath."

"Okay, I get that. Now, what you got?" asked Super Techie, her impatience more apparent.

"It's him, Mustafa Younan. It's him."

"Go back a step, Ali, so I can follow what you're saying."

"Okay. I'm okay. I believe he's the bomb maker. Equipment was stolen from one of the outreach science labs at his university when he was there; he also had ready access to everything he might need to make bombs. I've also used the facial recognition software and he's a constant visitor to the mosque. Added to that, in one of the pictures we were sent, he's in a very animated conversation with Nasir al Din Beshara. Isn't he a person of interest?"

"Yes, he is. Good job, Ali. I was phoning because there's nothing to link the fourth person on my list with what's going on. I'll pass the information you've found to Adrian immediately so that Younan can be picked up for questioning. Can you send me all the evidence, please?"

"It should already be with you. I forwarded everything I had."

"Thanks, Ali. I will get back to you once I know anything concrete."

"Okay. I'm still keeping an eye on the FfF website, but it's gone very quiet. Want me to continue with that?"

"Not a bad idea, Ali. Thanks."

***

Alan Edwards put the phone down and took a minute before he contacted Shihab Ozer's team. Following his conversation with Adrian Smythe, he was hoping that they could pick up Younan and stop any more fatalities as a result. The death of Muttaqi Saladin, one of his own, sat heavily on his shoulders. Alan would do everything in his power to stop anyone else being hurt. The conversation he had next with Shihab was short; the instruction being to pick up Mustafa Younan and bring him in for questioning. The added proviso was to be extra careful. If Younan was the bomber, his house could be booby-trapped. Within minutes, the team was on their way to the house in which Younan lived with his aging parents.

While members of the team were on their way to his

house, Mustafa Younan was putting the last things into his large rucksack. He had changed from his usual style of dress into the traditional garments, more often worn by older Muslims. A brief glance around his bedroom and then he walked down the steep staircase, thinking that he would most probably never see this house again. Younan wasn't bothered by that thought. He'd never liked the house but, as his parents had allowed him to live with them rent free, it had been convenient and he had enjoyed his personal space in the cellar. Being a selfish young man, full of his own importance, he gave no thought at all to what might happen to his parents if they were thought to be part of the group planning the bombings. They'd lived a long life and were old and, to his thinking, useless to him now. In his warped mind, he considered whatever would happen to them to be the work of the Prophet, so no blame could be his. Walking through the house, he went into the kitchen and out through the back door, which locked as he pulled it shut. Then, seemingly without a care in the world, he walked briskly down the alleyway behind the houses into his future, whatever and wherever that would be.

***

Jim Adams was the first person out of the car when it stopped at the end of the street where Mustafa Younan lived. Shihab Ozer and Maura Grainger were going to approach the front door, whilst Jim would go around the back of the houses to the back door, in case Younan tried to escape that way. Shihab would give Jim three minutes to get into position, and then he and Maura would walk up the street and knock on the door.

Shihab knocked and waited. Knocked and waited. Then

he shouted and knocked again; looked through the letter box and shouted, but got no response. Just as he turned to Maura to discuss the next course of action, he saw a grim-faced Jim Adams walking up the street towards them.

"Gone," stated Jim, his face stone.

"What do you mean gone?" asked Maura.

"I was walking up to the back door when I heard voices. It was two young boys playing in the alley. They asked me who I was looking for and while I was thinking what to say they told me Younan had gone."

"Just like that? They could have been lying. He could be hiding inside."

"No, I don't think so. While I was considering what to say, they told me the parents are away for a month visiting relatives and Younan had just walked down the alleyway. I walked up to the back door and looked in and there's no one there."

"Bloody hell! Snarled Shihab, his face was a picture of frustration and anger.

Maura put her hand on his arm, hoping to calm him.

"We win some, we lose some, Shihab. We all know that and it does hurt when we lose them. We'll get him eventually; we have to. You need to let Alan know now so he can put an alert out for him and get a search warrant for this house. We have no idea what Younan's left in there."

Shihab nodded, not trusting himself to speak, and walked back to the car to break the bad news to Alan. Jim made his way to the back of the house where he would remain until relieved. Maura waited by the front door, shoulders slumped, heart heavy.

***

The whiteboard in Adrian Smythe's office was a mass of information. He stood in front of it, adding, moving or erasing as necessary. He was at a point where he had to wait and see what happened next; not a place he liked to be. Even worse, he had to go and have a conversation with Mashuum Lodi, the grandad of the prospective bomber. The information he would have to impart to him would, Adrian knew, affect him deeply.

Adrian had phoned ahead and Mashuum was sitting in the interview room waiting for him.

"The news you have for me isn't good, I can see," stated Mashuum.

"No, it isn't, I'm afraid," replied Adrian.

Adrian proceeded to tell Mashuum that Dilawar had been found with the bombs in his rucksack. Mashuum wanted to ask questions, but Adrian asked that he wait until he'd told him everything. Mashuum had nodded that he would, so Adrian had continued to update him, including Dilawar's current state of health which wasn't good. Adrian told him about Abdul-Azeem Tawfeek's involvement and the evidence they were gathering about Mustafa Younan. Mashuum's pale, drawn face and eyes full of pain would haunt Adrian for ever.

"What can I do, Adrian? What can I do?" asked Mashuum.

"You need to go home — to your own home or your son's — and wait. You will need to support each other as the times ahead will not be good for you all."

"But we've done nothing wrong," Mashuum intoned.

"I know," stated Adrian wearily, "but people will always believe in guilt by association. You will have to be strong for

231

your family and hope what happens next doesn't make that impossible. We will catch the people involved in this, but it will take us some time."

"You will do your best, I know that, and I will try to do mine for my family."

"That's all that we can all do," stated Adrian.

Rising heavily from the chair, Mashuum left the room to collect his things and make his way to his son's house. Mashuum knew Qusay wasn't strong and would need all the support he could give him. Mashuum would do his utmost to be that strength for Qusay, despite the pain he, himself, felt.

Chapter Thirty-Seven

Cologne Cathedral was a mass of interaction: organised chaos would have been a good label for what was happening there. The visitors in the cathedral were unhappy about being confined to one area and not being told what was going on. They found the restrictive presence of the men in the hazmat suits worrying. There were lots of whisperings going on and furtive glances. One of the American visitors was more vociferous.

"I was in Vietnam: you knew when the men in the white suits were around, there was gas or something more lethal!" All this stated in a loud voice that echoed around the cathedral and increased the tension within. Before he could continue this tirade, HZ4 approached him, moved him to one side and leant into him, speaking quietly. Whatever HZ4 was saying had a serious effect on the man. Nodding his head and gesticulating in reply, the man then moved quietly back to his companions, head down and not making eye contact.

Outside the cathedral, three coaches were waiting. The windows of the coaches were coated in what was usually called modesty glass: you could see out of the windows, but no one could see in. Herded like cattle, the visitors to the cathedral trudged uncertainly to the coaches, boarded them and were quickly seated. An old, Japanese man seated near the front of the first coach asked for his phone to be returned. He was told it would be, in due course. The answer given in such a stern voice that it brokered no resistance. Within ten minutes, the coaches were on their way to an isolation centre outside the city where the visitors travelling on them would be vaccinated, then kept until it was safe to release them back into the public domain. Information would be taken from the visitors and relevant family members, hotels, travel operatives etc informed of an unavoidable delay.

Whilst this was going on, a large van was parked outside the cathedral, waiting for the coaches to move off. Once they'd gone, the lead box containing the two bombs was carried carefully to the back of the van. It was secured in the heavy safe inside so that it couldn't move around and wouldn't be affected by the change in road surfaces. The phone was taken to a different location where its contents could be interrogated without fear of detonating the bombs. The van containing the two bombs moved slowly away from the cathedral, with full police escort, along a route cleared of all traffic, to a facility outside Cologne where it was hoped the bombs could be defused without loss of life. Scientists from Porton Down had already been flown there, initially, to accompany the vaccine but, also, to be on site to help as they had experience of defusing the bombs from Sweden and were 'acquainted' with the bomber's techniques.

HZ1 was very worried about Dilawar Lodi's health. His vitals were erratic and his breathing was laboured. Had he been able to, HZ1 would have removed Dilawar before the bombs but, as the visitors were the innocents and Dilawar the guilty party, the visitors had to be removed first. Then it was the bomb, and then Dilawar. The medical staff, both wearing hazmat suits, entered the toilet area, did a quick check on

Dilawar and then indicated that a trolley should be brought in. Dilawar was placed on it, secured so that he couldn't fall off and then moved quickly into a waiting ambulance which was to follow the same route to the isolation centre. There he would be treated in the purpose-built medical wing, alongside any visitors who may show signs of reaction to the ricin or to the vaccination.

The cathedral's own security staff was gathered in the gift shop. They had been told what had been found in the cathedral, where it was found and that it had been removed. Standing in front of them was HZ2.

"Although we've removed two bombs, we can't be sure we've got them all. You know the cathedral and all its nooks and crannies, don't you?"

They all nodded.

"What we need is for you to go in pairs and check all the places you know. We've got sniffer dogs and their handlers to help but, without you, we could be wasting our time. If you're willing to help, we'll get the search done more quickly and we can then get you to the isolation centre for vaccination. What do you say?"

For a moment, there was silence, then Heinrich, one of the guards, put up his hand.

"Won't we be in danger?"

"I can't say you won't, I won't lie to you. We do think there were only two bombs so our search is just a precaution. However, if you don't feel you can help, we will do it on our own," stated HZ2.

After a couple of minutes, Heinrich spoke again.

"Okay, I'm in."

Heinrich stepped forward and, soon, the whole team was

behind him. HZ2 smiled, turned and walked back into the cathedral. He felt like the Pied Piper of Hamlyn with the string of people following behind him. Soon be over, I hope, he was thinking as he joined the group of dog handlers in the cathedral. The search was on!

**

Adrian Smythe was yet again standing in front of the whiteboard in his office in London. He'd just finished updating it and was looking at the links. He couldn't believe they'd missed Mustafa Younan who was, they believed, the bomb maker. Adrian had put out an alert on him, alongside the one for Nasir al Din Beshara but, as Younan didn't have a car or, it seemed, a mobile phone, he might be the more difficult of the two to find. The street Younan lived in had been evacuated and a team was checking inside the house. Obviously, they were suitably dressed in case Younan had booby-trapped his house. Adrian walked away from the board and sat at his desk. He was thinking that there must be a link he'd missed but, try as he might, he couldn't see it. He picked up his phone and was surprised to hear Ali's voice.

"Hi, Adrian, I tried to get Super Techie, but her phone's engaged, so I thought I'd give you a try," stated Ali.

"Give me a try?" asked Adrian, his mind momentarily elsewhere.

"Yes."

"Okay. What can I do for you?" he asked, stumbling over his words.

"Well, I'm still keeping tabs on the FfF website and there's someone on there I've struggled to identify. The IP address seemed to be diverted everywhere, but I've now got the source?"

"Okay."

"I'm sure it's a name I heard when we were looking for the bombs in Sweden."

At this, Adrian sat straighter in his chair, feeling that tingling at the back of his neck when a link was made.

"Said Turay. Does the name mean anything to you?"

"Say again, Ali."

"Said Turay. I'm sure I've heard the name before, but can't place where."

"That's the link, I bet. He's Beshara's cousin and he does all his travel arrangements. I don't know how we've missed it. I'll bet he knows where Beshara is. Great job, Ali. I owe you one!"

"No problem," replied Ali, feeling very pleased with herself.

Adrian was straight on the phone to Alan Edwards instructing him to pick up Said Turay. Perhaps he would lead them to Beshara. One can only hope.

Chapter Thirty-Eight

Arriving at his son's house, Mashuum Lodi took a deep breath to calm himself before he rang the doorbell. When Anna, his son's wife, opened the door, he could see the worry etched on her face. Looking at her, the stronger one, he dreaded how his son would look.

"Is Qusay here?" he asked.

"Of course, sorry, I was just surprised to see you. Why didn't you ring?" asked Anna. The look Mashuum gave her in reply, told her everything she needed to know.

"Dilawar?" she asked, in a voice trembling with emotion.

"You must be strong, Anna. You must be strong," Mashuum stated, gently patting her arm.

Walking up the hall to the lounge, Mashuum was shocked at what he saw there. Qusay was sitting on the sofa in what looked like a catatonic state: eyes glazed over, body stiff and barely breathing. It took Qusay a few minutes to register that it was his father standing in front of him.

"Dad!" he shouted, jumping up. "Where have you been? Where's Dilawar? What's going on?" spittle running down his chin, wetting the front of his top.

Mashuum didn't speak. He wrapped his arms around his son and held him until he felt Qusay's body go slack. Mashuum put him back on the sofa and sat down beside him.

"It's bad, my son. It's bad."

Mashuum took Qusay's hands in his and told him all he knew. When Qusay tried to interrupt, he put up his hand to stop him and then continued until he'd finished all he had to say. Qusay looked into his father's face and saw his pain reflected in his father's eyes.

"Not Dilawar. Oh, not Dilawar! I can't believe it. How? Who?"

So many questions and not enough answers.

"We must wait," said Mashuum. "Things are happening and we'll know soon enough. For now, we need to ask the Prophet for his help for, without that, all will be lost."

Mashuum stood up, orientated himself and dropped to his knees. He began to recite the prayers he knew so well, letting them wash over him and calm him. Without saying a word, Qusay knelt beside him and began to pray with him, as Anna slipped quietly out of the room.

***

The PM had not been happy when Adrian had facetimed her because the situation with the bombs was still a deadly one. She had, though, been in a better frame of mind than the last time Adrian had spoken with her. Bombs found, bomber still alive, but barely, and the threat at Cologne Cathedral contained. It could have been much worse. She asked that Adrian keep her up to date with any developments while she and the Chancellor of Germany were working out how to keep the situation out of the media. He wasn't at all sorry when the conversation ended.

In the interview room, Abdul-Azeem Tawfeek was sitting in

the chair, trying to look more confident than he felt. He had no idea what was happening outside and he'd lost track of how long he'd been incarcerated, so he was definitely wrong-footed. Adrian Smythe walked in and sat opposite him, his partner once again standing in the corner.

After five minutes, Tawfeek couldn't stand the silence any longer.

"Why am I here? I've done nothing. You must let me go!" his voice becoming more stringent as he spoke.

Adrian didn't reply. He stared at Tawfeek, never blinking nor losing eye contact. Tawfeek shuffled uncomfortably in the chair.

"Did you hear me?"

Nothing.

"Answer me!" this time his tone ripe with hatred.

Nothing.

Tawfeek's face grew redder and redder as he tried to maintain his equilibrium. At the point where he seemed about to erupt, Adrian spoke.

"You will be taken away and put in solitary confinement. Your crimes are the torture and death of Muttaqi Saladin and terrorist activities, involving the making and placing of bombs."

"You have no evidence of any of this! It's all lies! You hate me because I'm a Muslim! You're a racist!" he spat.

In his calmest voice, Adrian replied, "We have all the evidence we need about Muttaqi Saladin's torture and death. Your friend, Abdul-Alee Khatib, has been very helpful after his near-death experience. As for your terrorist activities, we've stopped your plans for the bombings."

"Bombings? What bombings? You talk in riddles! I am a

faithful Muslim!"

"Sweden. Cologne," was all Adrian replied.

Tawfeek gasped, and shrank back into his chair, deflated and unsure.

Adrian pressed a button under the table and two guards appeared at the door.

"Prepare him for his journey and let me know when he's arrived at his new destination."

"Yes, Sir," replied the smaller of the two guards.

They almost lifted Tawfeek out of the chair and moved him out of the room to get him ready for the next phase of his interrogation, after he'd been moved to his new location.

Once they'd left, Adrian left the room and made his way back to his office, where he felt the need to wash his hands intensely, as if he could wash away the evil that surrounded Tawfeek.

***

In the isolation centre in Cologne, most of the visitors to the cathedral had been vaccinated. An elderly American woman had reacted badly to the vaccination and had been removed to one of the medical isolation rooms, where she was being observed and treated. As a result, two of the Japanese visitors had refused the vaccination and were adamant that they would not have it, threatening legal action if they were forced to do so. These two were kept in medical isolation, too, in separate rooms.

Zaigham was also put into medical isolation. He had shared a room with Dilawar and, as there had been a minute leak of ricin from one of the Nalgene bottles which were in the rucksack in the room he shared with Dilawar, he was showing signs of a reaction to it. Blood samples had been taken from him before he was vaccinated and would be taken two days after. He was responding to treatment.

Dilawar was in a very bad way. He was linked up to various machines which were either monitoring his condition or administering medication or pain relief. He was severely dehydrated and his kidneys weren't functioning properly. Blood samples had been taken as soon as he was admitted and they were to be taken every thirty-six hours. No one was sure if he would pull through, but they were all doing their best for him. The worse thing was that his family couldn't visit or even know where he was being held. That was going to be very hard for them; particularly, when it became known he was a prospective bomber.

In Cologne Cathedral, the search for more bombs was almost done. The cathedral security staff was to be driven to the isolation centre where they would be vaccinated and kept for a couple of days to ensure they hadn't been contaminated. The cathedral would be kept out of action for seven days, so that checks could continue and the air conditioning systems could be inspected and cleaned.

Journalists had turned up near the cathedral and were desperate to find out what was going on. They were told nothing. Usually, someone would put something on Facebook or Twitter and the press would pick up any stories and run with them. As all phones had been confiscated, there were no stories. However, what would happen when the cathedral visitors were released was anyone's guess.

Chapter Thirty-Nine

Mr Johnson was not happy, not happy at all. By arranging for Jenny Evans of South East Today to be at Teynham School when the boys got back from their trip to Dunkirk and Cologne, he had shot himself in the foot. He wondered how he could extricate himself from the situation so that any blame didn't fall on him. It didn't take him very long to realise that Mrs Williams, the head of the school, would have to be the sacrificial lamb. Rather her than me, he thought to himself, picking up the phone.

In her office, Mrs Williams was trying to deal with the fallout of the telephone conversation she'd just had with the police in Germany. She couldn't believe that one of her boys could be a bomber, especially someone like Dilawar Lodi, who was such a good lad. Mrs Williams had spoken with Mr Johnson about the call, and he'd advised her to text all the parents to tell them that the boys had been delayed but would be home in a few days. She wasn't going to do that. The parents trusted her and she wasn't going to lie to them, for Mr Johnson or anyone, but what she was going to do, she didn't know.

As she picked up her direct line, she knew it wasn't going to be good news. It never was on that line. How right she was! Mr Johnson had informed her that she had to contact Jenny Evans at South East Today and tell her that the boys had been delayed, so they'd have to cancel her visit. He didn't say what to tell her about why they were delayed. She put the phone down at the end of the conversation and gave a large sigh. Mrs Williams had no illusion about Mr Johnson and his style of management. She knew as soon as she got the call that he would do his best to put any blame on her about the present situation — that was his modus operandi. What a prat, she thought, surprised at the intensity of her disgust.

Walking around her office, Mrs Williams decided to tackle Jenny Evans first. She would then text the parents to say the boys would be delayed, but call them to a meeting to discuss it. Mrs Williams wasn't sure what she would tell them but, by the meeting, she should have a better idea. She'd been told on the call from Germany that Dilawar's parents had been informed of the situation, so she decided to phone them before texting the other parents.

"Hello?" a frail voice.

"Hello. Mrs Lodi?"

"Yes. Who's this?"

"It's Mrs Williams from school."

"Oh!"

"I'm so sorry, Mrs Lodi, about the situation with Dilawar. Is there anything I can do? I will have to text the other parents about the delay coming home, but I will tell them as little as possible. I can't believe Dilawar was involved in what they told me."

There was no response, just a sob at the other end of the line and then, nothing.

***

Jenny Evans was very curious about Mrs Williams' call. The fact that she was not forthcoming about why the boys were delayed coming home intrigued Jenny, who decided to do a bit of online research to see if anything had gone wrong in Dunkirk or Cologne. If it had, there would be something on the internet, she was sure. Would it be an interesting quest or a waste of time? Jenny thought it would be interesting. She didn't know why. Perhaps it was because she'd tried to phone Mr Johnson about it, but he was unavailable, which gave her that tingly feeling when there was a good story to be had?

***

In Teynham, Anna Lodi put down the phone after speaking with Mrs Williams. She dreaded what was to come. She couldn't believe Dilawar was going to plant some bombs; bombs with a deadly chemical inside that would kill lots of people. Not just kill them, but give them a horrifying death! Anna couldn't remember the name of the chemical, but she knew it was something very, very bad. When you hear the phrase about feeling your heart break, Anna had always thought it was a bit over the top but, now, she knew exactly what it meant. Her life, Qusay's and Mashuum's had all been turned upside down by the recent events but, even worse, Dilawar was in another country, desperately ill and no one knew if he'd survive. They couldn't go to where he was because they didn't know where he was being kept. All they knew was that he'd reacted to the chemical in the bombs, and was critically ill and being cared for. Whether he would live or not was anyone's guess. How do you handle something like this?

***

Alan Edwards team had picked up Said Turay, who seemed surprised to see them. He made no comment when they told him they were taking him in and went with them without any fuss. Confident or arrogant?

***

The search of Mustafa Younan's house had been very interesting. The living areas of the house were as you'd expect and nothing untoward was found there. The cellar, though, was a whole new ball game. Locked doors with what was definitely scientific equipment and an NBS suit. The dogs went mad in there, but nothing was initially found to substantiate their reaction until a concealed door was found in the floor. In the crawl space, there were definite traces of ricin and a locked safe was going to be moved out of the space and taken to where it could be opened safely. No trace of keys or of the vast quantities of castor beans that were still unaccounted for. Younan may have put them in a lock-up somewhere, so they'd have to continue to look for that.

***

Dan was packing his rods and reels which he was taking to Spain on his fishing trip. He needed to see that the weight didn't exceed what he was allowed to take. Ali watched him, amazed at the care and precision that went into his preparations.

"How long will you be away?" she asked.

"Just a week. Go on Sunday, come back the following Sunday."

Let's hope you catch what you're hoping to catch," Ali stated, as she was leaving the garage area.

Ali was looking forward to her tai chi class the next day. She thought she needed the exercise and the meditative properties of tai chi were great. She was going to have 20 minutes on the new game she'd bought — Fortnite — and was looking forward to that new adventure, when her email pinged. It was Adrian Smythe asking if she could meet him at his office in London on Monday next week. He said he had a proposition to put to her. Did he now?

***

Adrian heard an email ping into his inbox as he was finishing the update on the ricin bombs and bomber. It wasn't complete yet because he had to wait and see what happened with Dilawar Lodi, the bomber, and all the others still being held in isolation, but he'd wanted to get a start on it. Beshara and Younan were still at large and he was going to interview Said Turay, later that afternoon. Hopefully, he'd get some leads there.

The email was a reply from Ali to his email asking her to come up and see him next week. He decided to leave reading it until he came back to the office. Adrian looked in the mirror, adjusted his black tie and made his way to his car. His driver would take him to the airport for his flight to Leeds. He was going to attend the memorial service for Muttaqi Saladin, a faithful Muslim and a true hero.